The Sands of Inishowen

John G Dilworth

Contents

Dedication

I would like to dedicate this book to my mother, Katleen Gallen, who had an extreme love of local history and poetry. She always claimed to be a descendant of the Spanish Armada. She was a native of that part of Donegal where the Gallen name is most common and remains so to this very day. A part of Ireland well within the orbit of Inishowen and Derry City. She produced her own book of poems, and while they were never published, they are a treasure that will live on in our hearts. In a way, she was the inspiration behind the 'Sands of Inishowen'

Acknowledgments

I would like to acknowledge my sister Marie Chichignoud, who compiled much of the ancestral information on the Gallen family, and also my wife Mary and daughters Sandra and Linda for their encouragement to persevere when the proverbial well ran dry.

About the Author

John Gerard Dilworth, son of an Irishman and Grandson of an Englishman. John's father was an electrical engineer in Donegal, where he met and married Kathleen Gallen, who always claimed to be a descendant of the Spanish Armada when one of their ships ran aground and sank at Inishowen on the north coast of Donegal.

John grew up in Ballyshannon, one of the oldest towns in Ireland, where he developed a deep appreciation and love of Irish history. With the increased interest in ancestry, John started to explore his own ancestry, especially on his mother's side. Lack of record keeping over the years made accurate information impossible. However, he found enough compelling evidence to suggest that his mother may have been right.

Some of the interesting facts that he uncovered were:

(a) In Ireland, the name 'Gallen' is predominantly found in north Donegal around the area of Inishowen, where the Armada ship the 'Trinidad Valencera' sank.

(b) The ship that sank was originally named the 'Balanzara' a Venetian cargo ship commandeered and renamed 'The Trinidad Valencera' by the Spanish King Philip II.

(c) The Name Gallen is said to originate from the town of St. Gallen in Switzerland, close to Venice, where the Balanzara was registered.

It was only after the sinking of the Trinidad Valencera that the name Gallen started to show up in local senses in Inishowen.

John Dilworth

Chapter One

Francesco

James was nine years old, and his brother Tony was eight as they watched the bodies of their parents placed on the blazing fire with the others. They were all gathered in the village clearing to dispose of the bodies. Mothers, fathers, sisters, brothers, young and old, the plague made no distinction. The smell of death and burning flesh permeated the air. It was a smell one could not escape from and one they would never forget. As the numbers of the dead grew, the burial and disposal of the bodies became a problem for the authorities. Initially, they dug mass graves until they started to run out of land and time as the bodies kept piling up. James held his brother's hand and squeezed it gently to reassure him that things were going to be all right. It had always fallen to James to look after his younger brother; he could never understand why. Tony was taller and stronger than he was, and he was also a better fighter. Earlier that morning, they stood at the end of the bed with masks covering their nose and mouths as they bade farewell to their dying mother. The last thing his mother said to him. "James, take care of your brother." Her voice was soft and weak, but he heard her just the same. She told them how much she loved them both, gasping with her last breath before she passed on.

This outbreak of the Bubonic plague, or the 'Black Death' as it was commonly called, was just one of several waves of the plague that hit

Venice and the surrounding areas since it first surfaced in Italy. Despite all efforts of the government to curtail the disease, it spread rapidly in the city of Venice and the surrounding farming communities, including the townland of Veneto, where the Gallen family worked their small farm holding. They had seen widespread sickness and death before, but never had they experienced anything on the scale or severity of this outbreak of the disease that swept through the whole community with such devastating speed. Some say it was originally started by Mongolian invaders in the Crimean city of Caffa, in the Republic of Feodosia, and was brought to Messina, Sicily, on Genoese merchant ships. They say that ships arrived in Messina from Crimea with everyone on board either dead or dying from the disease. Others say it was brought by merchant cargo ships that carried grain all over the Mediterranean. They say the grain was rat-infested, and the rats were infected with the plague, and when the rats died, the disease spread to humans. In any case, the plague spread quickly from one city port to another and eventually to the rest of Italy.

Nobody knew for sure how it was transmitted from one person to another or how it spread so swiftly through the community. Everybody had their own theory and suspicions. Some blamed the rats, and some blamed the water supply, while others thought fleas and lice spread it. When it eventually swept through the vulnerable city of Venice, it killed fifty to eighty percent of the inhabitants. The population of the 'Republic of Venice' dropped by over fifty thousand inhabitants in a matter of months. In an effort to slow the spread of the disease, the personal property of all those infected was burnt with all their possessions. As was James and Tony's home and the home of their closest neighbor, the 'de Marco' family, who lived on the adjacent farm, and so it was with so many others in their village. The people were getting used to death. They lost friends, neighbors, sisters and brothers, fathers and mothers. Nothing would ever be the same again. There was no end to their misery. There was little or no guidance or information coming from the government or the medical profession as to how people could protect themselves. The people were doing whatever they could to avoid the disease that was spreading like wildfire. The plague medics were protected with a long cloak, gloves, and boots. They wore a beaked mask specially designed to hold herbs and spices to protect them from the smell. Not wanting to use their hands, they also carried a cane to check the sick bodies for signs of the disease.

The city of Venice at the time was a veritable petri dish. It was a cesspool that assisted the spread of disease, and the plague was no exception. People kept animals in the city without proper hygienic housing and slaughter facilities. Sewerage was thrown out of windows and flowed down the middle of the street. Gentlemen walked on the inside out of courtesy to the ladies. Although the cause of the disease was unknown, the city of Venice was quick to realize that containment measures were their best hope to curtail the spread, especially in the densely populated areas. The City authorities set up a quarantine center on Lazzaretto Island to house those who were suspected of having the disease. Ships entering the lagoon were boarded and searched for sick or dead sailors. It was not unusual for sailors to get sick and die from any one of the many diseases that were common on-board ships, especially during a long voyage. If contamination was suspected, the ship was quarantined initially for forty days. If it was not cleared after that, it was detained in a quarantine station indefinitely. They fumigated the cargo with rosemary and juniper, the same herbs the medics used inside their beak masks for protection. They regulated and monitored the sale of wine, fresh meat, and clean drinking water by carrying out regular inspections. They did what they could to improve the sewerage system. They regulated the burial and disposal of the dead. Public drinking houses were closed down, not only to prevent crowds from spreading the disease but also to appease those who believed the plague was invoked by the wrath of God for illicit behavior by the patrons. A health pass was required to enter public places. Masks were mandatory. Whole communities were segregated. Despite all of these controls, it was every man for himself. Nobody trusted anyone and blamed everybody. Friends were lost forever, and families were torn apart.

The most common symptoms of the Bubonic Plague were painful lymph gland swelling around the neck, armpits, and groin that formed boils that oozed pus and blood called buboes, hence the name 'Bubonic Plague.' This was followed by the skin covered with dark blotches. Other forms of the plague were the pneumonic plague, which attacked the lungs first, and the septicemic plague, causing blood poisoning. The symptoms also included fever, difficulty breathing, vomiting, aching limbs, coughing up blood, extreme pain caused by decay or decomposition of the skin, extreme fatigue, gastrointestinal problems, delirium, coma, organ failure, hemorrhaging, and finally death. The dead were wrapped in sheets and left out in the street to be carted away and disposed of by order of the authorities. Nobody was given a proper Christian burial, no matter what the cause of death. It did not target any group in particular. It did not matter whether they were young or old, weak or strong, rich or poor. People fell ill and died within four to ten days of contracting the disease. No one was safe, and the worst part was the speed with which it spread through the community and left so much death and suffering in its wake.

Francesco, their father's brother, came down from the mountain when he heard about the plague to take the whole family back with him to a more remote region where they might be safe. It was too late for his brother Philip and his wife Maria, but hopefully, he was in time to get the boys to safety. Francesco had to be careful not to bring the disease back to his own community. He was very careful to keep a safe distance from everyone and everything. He wore gloves and a mask at all times. He had a complete change of clothing with him. His old clothes were burned along with everything he used or touched on his journey. The boys were stripped of every stitch of clothing, all of which was burned before they were scrubbed from head to toe, as was Francesco himself. The only clothes that Francesco could muster up on short notice were some spare robes that he borrowed from some of the young monks back at the monastery. They were made of a heavy woolen material that was tied around the middle. They were a little big for the boys, but they were warm, and with a little adjustment, they fitted just fine. He reassured the boys that proper and more suitable attire would be organized when they reached their new home in the mountain.

There were many others on the road trying to escape the plague. Mostly families and small groups who liked to keep to themselves, carrying their meager possessions on pushcarts or on their backs. Francesco was fortunate enough to have a mule and a small cart supplied by the monastery. Very few others on the road had the luxury of a mule-drawn cart. They walked for the most part, stopping only to rest and eat along the way. They came across a mother who had lost her husband to the plague and was struggling to take her young family to her sister's home in the country when the cart she was pushing broke a wheel. Nobody wanted to help her and risk infection. Francesco was also careful not to get too close, but he did give her the mule and cart to ease their burden. He blessed them and sent them on their way. He said it was no more than the good lord would have done. Groups of vigilantes gathered outside villages along the route in an effort to protect their community, not allowing travelers to stop or loiter anywhere in or around their village. They even resorted to violence and stone-throwing to scare people off. On seeing Francesco and the boys dressed as monks, they were less hostile and more tolerant for fear of offending the almighty. Some people believed God sent the pestilence to punish the wicked. While keeping a safe distance, they would offer food and water. The monks were known to solicit food, and most people liked to help them in the name of the lord. However, Francesco was a bit weary of getting too close to strangers and knew just how very contagious the plague was and feared being the one to bring the disease back to his community.

Living in the country and having served in the army, Francesco was an experienced survivor and well used to living off the land. He was used to fishing the freshwater streams, trapping wild game, and gathering fruit, nuts and mushrooms. These were the survival skills he would pass on to the boys when they were old enough to go camping with him. They lit fires to keep warm at night and cook whatever they could catch or sneer during the day. They sheltered from the rain and the elements, but most of all, they stayed safe from the pestilence that lurked all around them. Francesco's home was a secluded community in the mountains where the air was fresh and clean. A Franciscan Monastery nestled in the Alpine mountains of northern Italy. The monastery was founded by St. Francis of Assisi in the 15th century. It was a place of higher education, learning, and meditation for young men from all over Europe, especially young novices with a vocation for the priesthood. They would all have to isolate when they got there for at least a month or until they were absolutely sure they were not carriers of the disease.

Francesco and his younger brother, Philip, originally grew up on a collective farm on the outskirts of the town of St. Gallen in Switzerland. The town evolved from the hermitage of St. Gall, which was originally founded by an Irish monk in the sixth century and later became the Benedictine 'Abbey of St. Gall' in the middle of the eighth century. It was one of the first monastery university schools north of the Alpine border, where young men came from all over Europe to study. Their farm was in a valley high above sea level in the hills between Lake Constance and the mountains of the Appenzell Alps. It had a humid continental climate with short, warm summers and long, cold winters with lots of snow. They herded large numbers of sheep that thrived on the marshy grassland; however, it was not suitable for growing crops. They kept a limited number of cows for their own dairy needs. It was a co-operative farm where they shared the work and tended their flocks of sheep on common land. It was a hard life, and they struggled to make ends meet. They traded with other co-operative farms further down the mountain in the valley below for wheat, flour, wine, and other necessities. It was always their intention to move down to more fertile land whenever an opportunity presented itself. Francesco and Philip's parents both died of the fever when the boys were still in their teens. The two brothers continued to work the farm together with the help of their neighbors and the co-operative. Francesco, the eldest, was the more dynamic of the two. He was the more responsible, the one who always took charge and cared for his younger brother Philip after their parents died.

The family were devout Catholics, and the boys grew up in a very Christian home. It was a family that practiced their faith and prayed together, and like most families at that time, they hoped that someday one of their sons might join the priesthood. From a very early age, Francesco had aspirations in that regard and often talked about joining the monks. He had already spoken to the Abbot at the monastery of St. Gall about joining the community there. The one thing that held him back was his promise to his parents to look after Philip. Maybe it was better to wait until Philip was a little older and better able to take care of the farm and manage things on his own. As the years passed, the inevitable happened. Francesco met a young lady called 'Maria,' and he fell in love. Maria came from the Veneto region of Italy, about halfway between the city of Verona and Venice. She came from a small farming community and was visiting her grandparents in Switzerland when she met Francesco. They were making plans to get married and settle down when the conflict broke out between the Catholics and the Protestant Reformists in Switzerland. Francesco felt it was his duty to take up arms on the side of the Catholics. He and his longtime friend Michael Simone went off together to join the ranks of the Catholic army. It seemed that everybody's life was put on hold back at the farm. Philip took over the running of the farm with Marie's help.

The federation of Switzerland was deeply divided between the reformists under the leadership of Huldrych Zwingli, who was based in Zurich and had the support of a number of other cities, including Berne and Francesco's hometown of Saint Gallen. On the Catholic side, you had the five Catholic Forest cantons who aligned themselves with Austria to form a holy League. Huldrych Zwingli, the leader of the Reformation, convinced the Zurich city council to convert to the new protestant religion. Huldrych, believing that a clash between the two factions was inevitable, urged the city of Zurich to prepare for hostilities. Both sides took up arms, but the hostility ended without any battle being fought, resulting in the first 'Peace

Treaty of Kappel.' Peace did not last long, with extremists on both sides fanning the flames of hatred and mistrust. After the reformists introduced sanctions and threatened a food blockade, the five forest cantons with 8,000 men mounted a surprise attack against the city of Zurich.

Francesco and his unit were on a reconnaissance mission to check out the Zurich army defenses when they were spotted by the reformists, who, thinking it was an all-out attack, unleashed a barrage of cannon and musket fire. Francesco's unit was completely wiped out except for himself and his friend Michael Simone. They both escaped but with severe shrapnel injuries. Francesco got hit in the head and lower abdomen, while Michael's left arm was badly shattered. Michael somehow dragged himself and Francesco back to base camp, where they reported to the commander Provost Jauch of the Uri canton. Jauch, on realizing the weakness in the Zurich defense, led the attack, resulting in the defeat of the reformists and the death of the leader, Huldrych Zwingli. The Zurich forces were caught off guard and were not fully prepared to defend the city. There was confusion in the chain of command, and their army was ill-equipped and totally outnumbered. Within fourteen days, the reformists were defeated again at the battle of Gubel, and the second 'Peace Treaty of Kappel' was drawn up.

The Catholics had gained a very decisive victory over the reformists. Still, the reformation was already deep-rooted and remained very strong in many of the large cities, including Zurich and Bern. It was also very strong in Francesco's hometown, where the reformation was adopted by the humanist mayor of Saint Gallen 'Joachim Vadian.' The church in the cities of Schaffhousen, Basil, Bienne, Mulhouse, Berne, and St. Gallen, were secularized. Icons and images of the saints were not allowed, and the state took over the management and administration of all church property. Catholic nuns were pressured to leave the monastery. This was followed the following year by dissolving all monasteries in the territory and the revenue used to fund education and to help the poor. A failed attempt was made to dissolve the Abbey of St. Gall, which was a state of the Holy Roman Empire in its own right. Some cantons in Switzerland tolerated both Catholics and Protestants and of course, the five Forest Cantons remained Catholic.

As Francesco lay on his hospital bed, he wanted to write and say he was coming home. Coming home to what? Everything had changed. Things would never be the same again. He had spent weeks recovering from his injuries. It took months of rehabilitation for him to get back on his feet. How could he tell Maria that they could never have children? He felt like he had left his manhood on the battlefield. Francesco turned to the church for answers and somehow realized that joining the priesthood was what God wanted him to do. He spoke to the Abbot at the monastery and was welcomed into the brotherhood as a novice priest. Francesco would spend the next few years studying and preparing for the priesthood.

Chapter Two
Gallen

The Abbey of St. Gall remained catholic, but nobody could depend on how long that would last. Francesco was dedicated to the church and the Abbey but was not prepared to continue under the new Protestant administration. Iconoclastic riots forced Francesco and most of the monks to relocate to a Franciscan monastery across the Italian border in a secluded valley in the mountains near the northern town of Merano.

They took with them holy images and icons for safe keeping and protection. His new home was far away from the influence of the reformation in Switzerland and a little closer to Phillip and Maria. Francesco worked very hard as he helped the elderly abbot set up a new school. As time passed, he took over more and more responsibility and eventually, became responsible for the school's administration.

The Catholic Church, or more precisely, the religious houses of that period, played an important role as centers of education and literacy. They were the original universities, even though they were initially established as houses of prayer and a place where young men prepared to preach the word of God. Most of the teaching staff and professors transferred from the Abbey of St. Gall to join Francesco.

As the monastery at Merano became better known and its reputation as a school for higher education grew, many more young men joined. As time passed, the new novitiate became the preferred school of learning for students and novices from all over the surrounding countries of Germany, France, Austria, Switzerland, and Italy, and even as far away as Spain and Portugal. They came from all over Europe to study there. The monastery was not only a place of learning and training for the priesthood, but it was also a university for those lay students who could afford it.

They went there to study language, the arts, and science. Higher education was also made available to poorer students who had the proper aptitude and acumen. Basic schooling and literary skills were also provided to poorer students by the mandate of the Catholic Church.

In the early stages of the reformation in Switzerland, letters had passed back and forth between Francesco, Philip, and Maria, constantly updating them on the war. Suddenly and without any explanation, the letters stopped coming. Maria's letters came back unopened. She thought maybe he was killed or was lying unconscious and dying in a ditch somewhere.

Then, one day, a letter came addressed to Philip with no mention of Maria. The letter said he was preoccupied with the war and did not know when he would be able to get home, if ever. He told Philip that in the future, he would have to run the farm on his own. Maria refused to tell him she was carrying his child.

She would not marry him out of pity. If he didn't care for her enough to write, she would raise the child on her own. That fall, Maria gave birth to a baby boy and christened him James after Philip's father. Philip continued to support Maria and his brother's child. However, as time passed and with no sign of Francesco coming home, Maria and Philip grew closer together. They struggled to make a living on their small holding in St. Gallen. When Maria's father died, her elderly mother could not manage on her own, so they decided to move to Maria's family farm in her home town of Veneto.

The land was more fertile, making things easier for the both of them. They were known in Veneto as the family from Gallen, Philip, and Maria de Gallen. They wanted to get away from the conflict between the Catholics and the Protestants, but also because Maria was being treated as an outcast by their neighbors, who would whisper and gossip behind her back and spread rumors of her immoral behavior and of her having illicit affairs and a child outside of marriage.

Philip and Maria married the following year after settling into their new home. Maria's mother died in the fall of that year, and two months later, she gave birth to a second son. They called him Anthony, after her own father. Philip tried to keep in touch with Francesco, but the letters were few and far between. Philip and Maria invited him to come visit and celebrate their wedding and the birth of their sons, but Francesco always had a good excuse.

If the truth be told, Francesco could easily have taken the time to go down the mountain to visit his brother Philip and his wife, Maria. What bothered him most was the feeling he had let them both down. All those years, he wallowed in self-pity when he should have faced up to the truth and been more open. Philip and Maria both deserved to know the truth, and he kept it from them. He kept it from them to protect them. It's what he always did. If you think they can't handle the truth, you live a lie, or was it selfish pride?

When he heard about the plague in the village, he got permission to offer Philip and Maria the protection and sanctuary of the monastery, at least until the disease had passed. Now, they were both dead, and he was escorting James and Anthony to their new home. The journey back to the Monastery was long and arduous.

Nobody on the road wanted to have anything to do with strangers. They often came across small groups of people burying their dead, bringing back memories of the devastation and heart break they had just left behind. Francesco would always stop and say a prayer and bless those gathered there.

The monastery was located on high ground overlooking a beautiful scenic valley in the Alps near the border of Italy and Switzerland. It was protected on all sides by the mountainous terrain. There was only one way in and one way out.

The main entrance was fortified by high walls and an extremely heavy gate. It was in a remote area out of the way of marauding thieves and bandits who regarded a monastery as easy pickings. It was seen as a place of refuge from the plague, somewhere where people felt safe and could pray for its passing. Travelers had to camp outside the gates. The monks had increased the farm's productivity to cater to the increase in numbers.

They would offer any extra food and what other assistance they could afford to help those camped outside. There was no real protection from the disease, here or anywhere else, as had already been proved with many fortified houses along the way falling victim to the disease. Francesco knew that nowhere was safe.

Strict household rules were put in place regarding cleanliness, personal hygiene, and isolation. He was going to do everything in his power to protect those in his care, especially James and Tony, from the same faith that had killed their parents, his younger brother, and his wife, Maria.

Nobody complained about the seclusion or the problematic journey back to the monastery. All that mattered now was that the two boys were safe, or as safe as they could be. Francesco loved the Alps and promised James and Tony he would take them mountain climbing when they were older.

Now was a time to get them settled into some resemblance of routine and normality. Francesco decided the best way for the boys to get over their terrible ordeal was to keep them busy. There was quite a large community at the monastery. There was plenty to keep the boys occupied. They would continue to attend school.

Above all else, the monastery was a place of learning set up to train the young novices for the priesthood, and Francesco had arranged for a special curriculum for James and Anthony. They would have their chores like everyone else who lived in the monastery. There were four hundred acres of farmland and a winery to be maintained. There were also numerous workshops for those interested in carpentry, metalwork, arts and crafts, and even knitting and sewing.

There was an excellent library that was a fountain of knowledge and contained up-to-date information on almost every subject. It contained an archive for old manuscripts and also included a scriptorium used for copying and illuminating rare manuscripts by the monastic scribes.

The monastery had an excellent martial arts program run by a Buddhist monk, a Kung Fu master, all the way from the Shaolin Temple in China, who was visiting on a cultural exchange program. He provided instruction and practical training in Kung Fu and the very similar Japanese art of Karate. This was very popular among the younger students, and Francesco was sure this was where the brothers would burn up most of that youthful energy. Besides, it was a useful skill to have if ever they should venture outside the confines of the monastery.

There would be ample time for sport and recreation. There was lots of snow for skiing and hunting. Francesco wanted the boys to have every opportunity and experience that all aspects of monastic life in the Alps could provide. He would like them to follow in his footsteps and become priests, but for now, he focused on their education. He would do what he could to ensure they had a good start in life.

In the following months, the boys settled into their routines and got caught up on their schooling. Their studies included history, geography, science and math, Italian, Latin, Spanish, French, and religion. They were free to explore their new surroundings, and it did not take long before they got to know their way around every inch of their new home.

They made lots of new friends. The community was one big happy family. They enjoyed having friends their own age, if not a little older, with whom they could compete in sports and competitions, especially Kung Fu and martial arts. They learned to communicate as best they could with students from other countries, improving their language skills in the process.

They especially enjoyed helping on the farm. They tended the animals, looked after the sheep, fed and milked the cows, helped with the birth of calves and lambs, churned the milk, and made the cheese. They also liked to watch things grow. Each of them had their own vegetable garden.

They joined the other monks to harvest the crops and pick the fruit, grapes, and olives. They became very accomplished farmers. The monastery was self-sufficient, and while the monks were a mendicant order who took a vow of poverty, they worked hard to provide the basic needs of their community, much like the Cistercian order in France. St. Francis intended that his order would rely on hard work rather than alms for sustenance.

In the remote regions of the Italian Alps, they provided for themselves and gave generously to those who sought their help and assistance. The Monastery was also associated with many of the higher educational institutes of Europe during this period.

The monk's life was not always an easy one. They worked long hours in the upkeep of the monastery, whether in the fields or the many workshops. Every monk had his chores, even James and Tony. However, there was ample time for sport and recreation. They enjoyed leisure and downtime to read or pursue their hobbies. One thing the monks did well was eat.

They had three meals a day. Breakfast started at five in the morning, with oatmeal, bread and cheese, eggs, and fruit. Lunch at noon consisted of stew, meat, and vegetables, Bread and cheese, milk or wine. Evening meals usually consisted of bread, cheese, fish, fruit, and wine. Snacks and fruit were always available throughout the day.

Everything they ate was home grown and produced by the monks themselves. After their evening meal, the monks, especially the younger men, would sit around for hours and tell stories about the great explorers and discoveries of new lands far across the oceans. Tales of treasure ships and pirates. Primitive people with different languages, customs, and beliefs. Strange birds, animals, and fruits like they had never seen before.

All this mind-boggling information transcended the barriers of language and communication. The other topic high on their need-to-know list was girls. They were getting to that age when their interest in the opposite sex took up more and more of their time.

As expected, the monastery was also a house of prayer. The brothers partook in all the religious services of the monastery. There were morning prayers, mass, and rosary every day—Thanksgiving before and after meals. In the evening, there were vespers and Stations of the Cross. Both brothers had quite good singing voices and took great pride in knowing the words of all the Hymns and would try to drown out the others. They also served as altar boys.

They memorized the Latin for the mass. Not only did they learn to speak Latin, but they also understood it. They fit right in and were well-liked by the community. They were also very much at home on the mountain and became quite expert in mountain climbing. They spent hours in the gym and practiced hard, perfecting their skills in the martial arts.

When they were free, they liked hiking in the countryside and took a keen interest in nature. Francesco would spend hours with them on the mountain. He was an exceptional climber, always emphasizing the importance of safety on the slopes. He taught them first aid and rescue skills. The monks formed a rescue team and were often the first responders in the hour of crisis. As the brothers grew older, they, too, became part of the rescue team.

In time, Francesco came to regard the boys as his own. He suspected he was James's real father but did not see any point in reliving the past. As far as he was concerned, he was now the father to both the boys and encouraged them in every way to come to him with any or all questions they might have. The months rolled quickly into years; it was not long before Francesco had two young men on his hands.

As the brothers started to move through their teenage years, Francesco couldn't help but notice changes in their physical development. They began to grow facial hair, and he could detect a change in their voice. Their voices were about an octave lower. He could always pick them out when singing in church. While they still had beautiful, deep tenor voices, they were noticeably a pitch lower. All of a sudden, they seemed to be taking a growth spurt.

As the months passed, the increase in testosterone levels was evident more than ever; they were a lot more competitive and boisterous in the gym. There was no doubt about it: they had reached maturity.

There was little or no opportunity for the two brothers to meet girls in the monastery, and while Francesco was responsible for their upbringing, he understood the importance of their exposure to the outside world. He discretely placed some literature around explaining the nature of sex and what was happening to them physically. He knew that sooner or later; he would have to set them free to explore the world on their own.

Meanwhile, his job was to make sure they were well prepared to set out on that journey. James was the more responsible of the two. As a young man, he was the one who had to take charge and was always relied on to do the sensible thing. He was never one to take chances. He would take a calculated risk when he had to, but not before weighing up all his options.

He was not a risk-taker. People always relied on his common sense to do the right thing. He read a lot, anything he could get his hands on. He liked a good adventure story, especially if it involved pirates and hidden treasure. He had a keen interest in wildlife and would hunt and trap with Francesco every chance he got. He also liked to fish and live off the land.

James was growing into a handsome young man. He had black shoulder-length hair, brown eyes, and sallow skin that always seemed to be tanned. He was very protective of his younger brother Tony. Although Tony was younger, he was the taller of the two by at least three inches. Both were very fit, but Tony was broader and stronger, while James was more skillful in the art of self-defense.

Tony was tall and handsome with a big head of curly red hair, blue eyes, and light skin from his mother's side. In contrast, James liked to dream and read about adventure. Tony was the more adventurous of the two and wanted to live life to the fullest in a more carefree way without all the responsibility it might entail.

They were as close as any two brothers could be; they fought each other's battles and covered up each other's shortcomings. They regarded and loved Francesco as a father, and he was always happy to help them with any problems. He was always hoping that one or both of them might follow in his footsteps and take an interest in becoming a priest. He even taught them the liturgy of the mass, which they seemed to enjoy.

The one thing that fascinated James more than anything else was exploration of the Americas, even more than mountain climbing. He knew a sailor's life was hard, but he had decided that this was what he wanted to do.

Francesco was not totally disappointed as he believed that God works in mysterious ways and needed people to sail around the world, carry the faith to these new lands, and convert them to Christianity in the name of Jesus Christ.

As James got older, he got more and more taken with the idea of becoming a sailor. He spent hours in the library reading about ships, their construction, and how the sails worked. He was fascinated by the great voyages of the fifteenth century by Portuguese and Spanish explorers like Christopher Columbus, Ferdinand Magellan, and Vasco da Gama, opening up a new route to India and the Spice Islands, the discovery of America and the circumnavigation of our world, spreading western civilization and Christianity.

He had a good tenor voice and liked singing hymns with the others at prayer meetings; he took a particular interest in composing 'sea-related work songs or shanties. These were songs with simple lyrics and a catchy beat, often without rhyme or reason. These chants or shanties helped to unite workers and crew in a single rhythm, making them feel part of something bigger than themselves, getting them to pull together, making light work of a heavy task, such as raising the anchor, hoisting the sail, or scrubbing the deck.

James often made up his own, one he could use while working on the farm, saving hay, or bringing in harvest. The other monks would always join in and sing along, whether it be James's shanties or Hymns, which they all knew, all with the same effect of making light of their monotonous and uneventful daily chores.

When he was high up on the face of a mountain, hanging by a thread, he liked to sing at the top of his voice to the echo of the mountains. He had a powerful voice and enjoyed nothing more than chanting the hymns at vespers. One of his favorite hymns was 'A ship is coming laden,' an analogy of the advent message. He would dream of being up on the ship's highest mast with the sea breeze blowing in his hair.

A ship is coming laden

There comes a galley, laden

Up to the highest board:

She bears a heavenly burden.

The Father's eternal word.

She sails on in silence,

Her freight of value vast

With Charity for mainsail,

And Holy Ghost for mast.

The Sands of Inishowen

The ship has dropped her anchor'

Has safely come to land:

The Word eternal, in likeness

Of man, on earth does stand.

At Bethlehem in a stable,

To save the world forlorn

O bless Him for His mercy

Our Savior Christ is born

Chapter Three

Venice

James and Tony knew that they first had to go to Venice, the most important shipping port on the Mediterranean. This was the place to start if they wanted to sail the seven seas. If they could only manage to get on a ship there, they hoped that one day, they might eventually get to sail with one of the great explorers. After much pleading with their uncle, the two boys went to Venice to pursue their dream of becoming sailors. Francesco knew they were ready to face the world wherever their journey might take them. He blessed them both and insisted they each take a small bottle of holy water with them to protect them on their journey.

They had enough provisions with them for a few days, and his last words to them were to be sure to write and remember their way home. It took James and his brother over a week to reach Venice.

They lived off the land and foraged for food wherever they could. They offered their services to farmers along the way for food and a place to spend the night. Farmers often looked the other way when a few eggs or even a hen went missing. They were well used to living rough and camping out.

On a few occasions, a local farmer allowed them to sleep in the barn or the hay shed. They collected fruit, nuts, and mushrooms on the way, trapped and fished wherever possible.

Francesco had given the brothers the contact information of his old friend Michael Simone, who operated a guest house in Venice, the 'Residenza Veneziana.' Michael promised to do whatever he could to help James and Tony when they were in Venice. He would get accommodation for them and show them around the city. Michael Simone was a boyhood friend of Francesco. They lived on neighboring farms. They went to the same school together, played together, and when they were old enough, they went mountain climbing together.

When Francesco and Philip's parents died, the brothers were still very young; it was Michael's parents who helped them carry on. They were always there to help, sharing their farming knowledge and experience with Francesco and Philip. They told them when it was time to sow seed and when it was time to harvest the crop. How to care for the animals and manage the farm, and were always there to lend a helping hand.

When Michael slipped and suffered a broken ankle out on the mountain in a blizzard, it was Francesco who stayed and took care of him until help arrived. They joined the army together and always had each other's back during that time. They confided in each other, and there was no one Francesco could trust more to look after his two boys.

When James and Tony reached Venice, they met up with Michael. He had organized a place for them to stay, close to the docks. After settling into their accommodation, they spent the whole day with Michael, who showed them around the city. He pointed out the places of interest, especially the waterfront area.

He told them how to stay safe, the places to avoid, where not to go alone after dark. Good places to dine or to have a glass of wine. The city can be treacherous, not unlike any other port city on the Mediterranean. Over the years, Michael got to know a lot of the sailors who stayed at his guesthouse when they came ashore after a long voyage and wanted to freshen up and sleep in a clean bed. He arranged a meeting for James and Tony with the master of the 'Balanzara,' which was currently tied up in the lagoon. The ship was only a few years old, an 1100-ton galleon, a merchant sailing ship owned by the Grand Duke of Tuscany.

The word on the street was that they were currently looking for sailors; they were always looking for good seamen. Michael passed on their personal information to the captain 'Horatio Donai.'

In the meantime, the two brothers spent their days soaking up the atmosphere in the beautiful city of Venice, the city of canals, Queen of the Adriatic, with its sheltered lagoon harbor, a perfect port for the Venetian merchant and naval shipping fleets. A city built on 118 islands connected by some 400 bridges.

La Serenissima; the capital of Venice's sovereign state and the most powerful merchant trading city on the Mediterrancan. The wealthy Venetian merchants influenced the financial markets of Europe. The city had its own currency, which was respected and sought after throughout the European economy and the shipping industry.

This city was the birthplace of the great explorer Marco Polo, who is credited with setting up the Silk Road to China. It is also the home of Vivaldi and Benedetto Marcello, the great baroque composers, another passion of James, who loved classical music. The city of Venice was foremost in Renaissance architecture and art with painters like the master Titian.

It was one of the wealthiest cities in Europe and the Mediterranean. In the early years, Venice prospered from trading salt produced at 'Chioqqa' in Venice. At one time, salt was so important it was often referred to as "white gold."

Having grown up in a monastery, James and Tony had never seen so many beautiful women. They felt like kids in a candy store. They had often discussed their strategy in asking a lady out on a date, yet they did not have any witty one-liners, nor did they have a clue how to approach and strike up a conversation with a pretty girl.

They were very self-conscious of their experience or lack thereof in this aspect of their lives. They did not want the girls to know they were brought up in a monastery. They were both very handsome young men, well-educated, athletic, and polite, and now they were about to embark on the adventure of a lifetime; who doesn't love a sailor?

James and Tony were both a little nervous about meeting the ship's master the following morning. Their future hopes and dreams depended on making a good impression. They knew there was a demand for sailors because of the ongoing war with the Turks and hoped their lack of experience would not work against them. The Turkish fleet was constantly at war with Venice. The Turks attacked and destroyed the city of Limassol and butchered its inhabitants.

In 1570, they launched a full-scale invasion in the Mediterranean. After the fall of the cities of Nicosia and Famagusta on the Island of Cyprus, the naval forces of the Holy League, composed mainly of Venetians, Spanish, and Papal Ships, defeated the Turkish fleet at the Battle of Lepanto. The significance of these events, together with the plague and the war with Turkey, had created a demand for sailors in Venice. James and Tony hoped this would be to their advantage when meeting with the ship's master.

James and Tony finally arrived and got their first glimpse of the 'Balanzara,' the ship they hoped would soon be their new home. She was a sight to behold; it was everything they had imagined she would be as she stood tall in the water, the sailors scurrying up and down the rigging, tending to the sails.

She had four masts: the Bonaventure mizzenmast with typical lateen rigging, and right next to it, the slightly taller main mizzen also lateen rigged with its triangular sail. At the center of the ship were the main mast and the foremast with square sails, four spars tall, lower, top, topgallant, and royal. James estimated they were forty or fifty feet high. He was used to climbing such heights and even higher on the mountain rock faces back home.

The steward took them to meet Captain 'Horatio Donai' and the ship's master, who greeted them well and agreed to a trial period of six months, and by then, he would have a better idea of what they were capable of. Their pay would be 10 lire a month to start, plus meals and board, which was acceptable to both brothers.

Considering their age, experience, and schooling, the captain decided to dispense with the usual five-year initial apprenticeship, but everything depended on their progress over the next six months. Both brothers would soon be over twenty, making them eligible for a sailor's license. James and Tony had made up their mind they were not going to mess up this opportunity.

The way things normally work on board ships, newcomers who are not trained as officers have to work their apprenticeship under the guidance of an older, seasoned, experienced sailor. They would usually start at the age of fourteen or fifteen years old, and for the next five or six years, they become the unpaid lackey of their mentor and suffer all kinds of abuse.

When they reach twenty-one years, they become full-fledged, able seamen in their own right. The brothers will need to learn everything they need to know about sailing. They will not be expected to do the more mundane tasks usually reserved for the younger apprentices, like swabbing the decks, Careening and scraping the barnacles and mussels off the hull, and catering to the needs of the able-bodied seamen.

The captain must have received the letter of introduction from the monastery. Here, he had two well-educated young men capable of reading and writing, of excellent character and education, conversant in more than one language, certainly officer material, and deserving of the master's special attention, especially with the current shortage of good men. Fast-tracking the apprentice process will require special permission, but the church was very influential in such matters. God works in mysterious ways.

The captain gave Dino, an experienced, able-bodied seaman, the task of providing the brothers an orientation tour and teaching them the skills required to sail an 1100-ton merchant ship. Dino was also tasked with introducing the two newcomers to the rest of the crew, showing them to their quarters, and getting them settled in. You might say to show them the ropes.

The ship would not be sailing for a few days, allowing them a few extra days to get to know their way around the city. The brothers expressed their gratitude and made their departure. They would report for duty Monday morning at 5 am sharp, and Dino would meet them at the gangway and start them on a period of orientation, which would last a week or until they got to know their way around.

They headed back towards their guest house, stopping at a nearby inn to get a beer and something to eat. Tony caught the eye of two pretty young ladies who had given more than a passing glance in their direction. He returned the glance and was surprised to get a smile, which he immediately returned.

Tony invited the ladies to join them for a drink, which they accepted. The introductions followed, and they agreed to share a meal together. The girl's names were Maria and Rosa, both gorgeous and charming young ladies. After dinner, the night still being young, they all took a stroll in the park. After the hot day, it was refreshing to feel the cool sea breeze on their face as they walked hand in hand in the shade of the sycamore trees. The two young men were in awe at the sweet softness of their touch and the cheerful laughter in their voices.

The sweet, fruity, spicy, and nutty fragrance of the sycamores was in the air, and a woman's scent was stirring a feeling inside them that sent hormones cascading through their veins. The next moment, throwing all caution and shyness to the wind as their bodies drew close and with eyes closed, their lips met in a sweet, passionate embrace as the couples held each other tight. They will always remember a moment of utter bliss as they experienced their first kiss.

The following day, Maria and Rosa decided to show the boys some of the sites of Venice. The city is famous for its Grand Canal, and what better way to travel than on a romantic gondola, a flat-bottomed rowing boat well suited to the shallow waters of the Venetian canals. The day was hot and sunny, with a slight breeze cooling the air as they lay back in the shade of the tendalin as the gondoliere, dressed in his red and blue striped shirt and red neckerchief and his wide-brimmed straw hat, maneuvered his craft through the flotilla of sightseers on the canal.

James marveled at the mobility of the gondola and how the gondoliere had complete control of the boat with a single oar, slow, fast, backward, forward, stopping, and turning. This guy should be captain of a ship, he thought to himself. They followed the canal until they came to the famous 'Piazza San Marco' or St. Mark's Square, with its stalls and markets, the biggest and most important square in Venice. They were amazed by the sheer splendor and magnificence of the architecture and buildings. Chief among these was St. Mark's Basilica with its ornate interior and the Doge's Palace, home of the Duke of Venice.

They stopped at a roadside café and watched as the world passed by, and they thought what a wonderful city it was. As it turned out, the girls worked locally and stayed in the same guesthouse as James and Tony. They all agreed that they would like to see more of each other, and that was how their friendship started, a friendship that seemed to grow stronger with every day that passed.

The two boys forgot their inhibitions, and in no time, they had become very comfortable in their new found friendship that developed into a deep and loving relationship with Maria and Rosa.

James and Tony got up early on Monday morning, full of excitement and anticipation, and made their way down to the harbor front, which was already buzzing with activity.

They met up with Dino at the gangway. They were carrying their sea chests with their personal possessions, as was requested by Dino. He showed them to their quarters and settled them in before taking them for a walk around the ship. They were introduced to each of the crew. They tried hard to remember all the names and faces.

It suddenly happened while they were being introduced to the crew: three faces staring back at them, like ghosts from the past, the 'de Marco' brothers Jacques, Carlos, and Luigi. They were older now, but their faces were unmistakable, even after all those years. Luigi gave a little chuckle, and Carlos gave a little smile while Jacques had that unmistakable sneer of discontent all over his face. The 'de Marco's' had a long-standing feud with the Gallens.

They were the worst of neighbors, working the adjoining farm to the Gallen's in Veneto. After their mother Veronica died of the fever, their father 'Lorenzo de Marco' blamed James and Tony's parents 'Philip and Maria,' being newcomers, for bringing the fever to their community. There was no proof of that, but everyone was suspicious of everyone else and accused others for no reason at all—a madness brought about by the plague.

After his wife died, Lorenzo turned to the drink and spent more time in the alehouse than looking after his farm. He neglected his farm and his children. He liked to blame the Gallens for his misfortunes and his own shortcomings. He accused Philip of poisoning the water supply when his cow was found dead in a drain. He blamed Philip's dog when dogs from the village chased his sheep to the point of exhaustion and death.

Philip always kept his dog tied up at night for that very reason. Lorenzo's sons grew up disliking the Gallen boys, which their father nurtured. Growing up, James and Tony, who were much younger, were constantly harassed and bullied by the 'de Marco' brothers. Their father, Philip, who sympathized with Lorenzo's plight, told his sons to avoid trouble and to stay out of their way as best they could.

When Philip and Maria died of the plague, so did Lorenzo. His three sons went to their uncle's home for a while, but later reports suggested all three had joined the Navy and had fought in the war against the Turks. There was no doubt they were excellent sailors and were more than capable of taking care of themselves.

On seeing James and Tony, Jacques, who always spoke for the other two, remarked under his breath, "So the captain's little pets have come to join us. Don't expect us to babysit them." James read the message loud and clear. James and Tony were not little school boys anymore, and having braved many a rock face on the mountains while at the monastery, fear was not in their nature, and with their self-defense training, they were equal to any challenge the 'de Marco' brothers could bring. However, they would be constantly on their guard and knew it was only a matter of time before trouble would find them.

Jacques liked everyone to think he was the leader. He liked to wield his dagger, showing off how skillful he was with the weapon. The left-hand dagger was about fifteen inches long with an ivory grip, double-fullered blade, and crucifix hilt with bent-down quillons. It was a magnificent dagger, and Jacques would spend his spare time witling a piece of wood when he wasn't throwing it and sticking it in the mast.

Jacques was popular among the crew and seemed to be their spokesperson. The crew was hostile towards James and Tony and never missed an opportunity to let them know they did not agree with their special treatment and that they were not welcome on board their ship.

This only made the two brothers more determined to succeed and prove they were up to the challenge, to make the most of the great opportunity they were being given. The hostility of the crew did not bother them because they knew the crew would eventually come around, and in the meanwhile, the two brothers would always be watching out for one another.

Chapter Four
Thieves and Pirates

There were two main trade routes a merchant sailing ship would take out of Venice.

One was the northern route from Venice to Constantinople and up the Black Sea to Crimea. The other was the southern route from Venice, south to Sicily or the island of Crete. They would also visit Alexandria and Cairo in Egypt to meet the Arab caravans coming from China and India with silks and spices. They would usually call on other ports along the way, including Jerusalem, Damascus, Bagdad, and finally, Cyprus on their way home to Venice.

On this, the first voyage for James and Tony, the ship sailed directly to Cairo to pick up a cargo of dates and ancient Egyptian artifacts and to meet the Arab caravan returning with Spices from India. On the way back, they would pick up a cargo of grain in Jerusalem.

Theft was common among the crew, and the penalty was severe. Stealing spices and other valuables and selling them on the black market was a very lucrative business. Thieves were highly organized and formed syndicates, with accomplices among the officers and the dock workers, enabling them to get rid of the stolen property quickly. The captain knew there was nobody he could trust among the crew. He regarded James and

Tony as two men of character with a religious upbringing who might prove to be loyal and trustworthy.

For this reason and this reason alone, the two brothers were given a slightly higher security clearance that allowed them to work in highly secure areas where valuable cargo was stored. The crew was also aware of this and avoided any contact with the two brothers. The ship's crew and their sea chests and belongings could be searched at any time while they were still on board.

A thief could not keep the stolen property in his possession for long and had to get it off the ship as fast as possible. The thieves would be warned beforehand of searches from corrupt officers, making it very difficult and almost impossible to catch them.

Thieves would steal the merchandise, usually spice, which was worth its weight in gold on the black market, and stash it somewhere on the ship until the heat died down when they could safely move it ashore. All crew members and their carryalls were searched upon leaving the ship.

The most common way to get stolen property off the ship was to hide it in the sacks of grain. They would open the sack and pour out some or most of the grain, leaving enough at the bottom to give the right effect and feel if checked.

They would fill the middle with the stolen goods and then refill the rest of the sack with grain. Anyone checking the sack would look in and see nothing but grain. When the sack left the ship, it was taken to a designated place to be retrieved later by the thieves. The operation required accomplices both on and off the ship. Most seamen stayed on board the vessel while it was docked, while others liked to visit their families and frequent the alehouses and whorehouses after a long voyage. Security was strict on all levels of the ship, but theft remained a major problem despite the efforts of the officers to stamp it out. There were simply not enough honest officers on board to police a ship the size of the 'Balanzara.'

Dino kept the brothers busy for the first few days, working in the storage areas below deck. Packing sacks of grain, storing barrels of merchandise, making sure barrels were secure and battened down. Spices and other valuables were sealed in barrels and stored in a special, secure room below deck. There was so much to learn, so many things to remember. Apart from Dino, no one else on board had the time or inclination to teach the newcomers, especially as they received special privileged treatment.

The Quartermaster and his helpers are responsible for the safekeeping of the entire cargo. Anything that cannot be locked away is guarded at all times. Security of the cargo was paramount on board a merchant ship, and to protect the vessel from hostile attacks, whether they came from the Turks, the Genoese, Pirates, or Arabs, the ship always carried a security detail of fifty to a hundred gunners and sharpshooters. However, it was theft among the crew that was causing the most concern.

All cargo had to be stored properly, and the weight evenly distributed throughout the ship for the voyage home to Venice. Food supplies, water, beer, wine, and valuables were stored in wooden barrels which were tightly sealed and waterproof. A team of coopers on board was responsible for maintaining the barrels. The grain usually accounts for the bulk of the cargo and needs more space. It is usually stored in a separate area below the deck.

Grain is usually stored in sacks that are easier to store, handle, and account for, as well as a way of controlling rats. When it reaches the port, the grain is transferred to a warehouse before it is redistributed by land or sea to other cities. Grain does not require much security as it is too bulky for the average sailor to steal.

The ship's master had been complaining a lot lately about theft among the crew, and security had to be stepped up. The captain, who would often turn a blind eye to the crew doing a little personal business on the side to supplement their merger wages, was now tightening up on security. He was anxious to stamp out organized crime even if he had to search every inch of the ship.

This made many sailors nervous, forcing them to get rid of any stolen property that might still be in their possession, and the faster they got rid of it, the better.

After a long day, James and Tony were glad to go ashore. They needed a little time away from the ship to relax and get their feet back on solid ground, if only for a few hours. They looked forward to meeting Maria and Rosa and having a quiet drink in the local inn. The inn was crowded, as expected at that time of the day.

Sailors were arriving and leaving from many of the ships tied up along the docks. They got a table close to a window and sat down. James was not surprised to see the 'de Marco' brothers and some other crew members sitting in a far corner of the alehouse. However, he was surprised to see Dino drinking with them. James distinctly remembered Dino saying he did not trust Jacques and his gang and warned James and Tony to stay clear of them. What was he up to now, drinking and joking with the very same people?

According to Maria and Rosa, Jacques and his comrades were regular customers. They were well-known as big spenders who made a lot of noise. They were also known as troublemakers and should be avoided. James and Tony, however, were not going to be intimidated by the 'de Marco brothers.' They were not school boys, not anymore.

On this occasion, Jacques and his friends were getting loud and could be heard all over the inn. Jacques approached the bar and started talking to Maria. He seemed to be hitting on her, and she was shrugging off his advances.

That was when Tony stepped in and politely asked him to leave her alone as she was with him. However, Jacques was not prepared to let things go.

"What are you going to do about it"? He asked as he went to poke him in the chest with his finger.

Tony was younger than James, but he was taller and more robust, and as Jacques went to poke him, Tony grabbed him by the fingers, and Jacques was forced to the floor as he called out in pain to his brothers for help. His brother Carlos rushed to his aid, a big backer guy wielding a knife. James jumped to his feet to intercept Carlos. Before he could trust the blade at Tony, he raised one leg high in the air, and with one leap, he landed a kicking blow to the side of Carlos's head and landed him flat on his face.

The brothers did not want to continue this fight in front of the ladies and asked Jacques if he had enough. Jacques's pride had taken a blow, and not knowing what they were up against, they quickly picked up their bags and hurried out of the alehouse, uttering abuse and threats at James and Tony under their breath.

On their way out of the alehouse, Carlos stumbled, dropping his shoulder backpack and letting the contents fall out. A large bag of spice burst open and spilled out over the floor. He cleaned it up fairly quickly, but before he left, his eyes caught James's, and they both knew the other knew the spice was stolen. Dino and the others had left at the first sign of trouble, and James was left wondering if Dino knew Jacques and his friends were spice thieves and if he was involved with Jacques in some sort of syndicate.

Just how many others were involved, and who could they trust? It was not going to be long before they found out. The following day, Tony was helping Dino in the storage room below deck. Around noon, Dino left Tony alone to tidy up and lock the store room, which contained all sorts of valuables. Later that day, Tony was called before the ship's captain, where Dino accused him of stealing an Egyptian statue of the Goddess Bastet.

When the security officer searched Tony's Sea chest, he found the statue among his possessions. Tony protested his innocence and claimed that he had been framed, but nevertheless, he was taken away and locked up below deck.

James pleaded Tony's innocence to no avail. The statue was found among Tony's possessions in his sea chest. The captain was stunned, but for the moment, he had to go with the evidence, and there was proof enough of Tony's guilt for now. The crew knew better than to leave their sea chest unlocked; they would always lock their chest, but James and Tony had nothing of value and didn't see any point in locking their chest.

Back in the monastery, they trusted everyone to respect their privacy; no locks were necessary. James sent word to his uncle in the monastery telling the whole story, what had transpired in the alehouse, the story of Dino in the pub, the spilling of the stolen spice by Carlos, the treats the de

Marco brothers made under their breath. The following day, on hearing the full story, the captain promised to reexamine the whole affair with an open mind.

On the captain's orders, a thorough search of the crew's quarters and belongings was to occur as soon as possible. He especially mentioned the quarters of the 'de Marco' brothers. Anybody leaving the ship was to be stopped and searched along with any baggage they may be carrying. When Dino was later asked about the stolen property, he explained how he left Tony in the store room alone. When he returned, he noticed one of the barrels had been tampered with, and he immediately reported the missing statue of the Egyptian Goddess Bastat. Tony was the last person in the room, and when he was searched, the missing piece was found in his sea chest. When asked how he opened the locked chest, he explained the key was still in the lock. The captain thought it strange that someone would leave stolen property in an unlocked chest. It made no sense! Dino was one of the few seamen on board able to write, so he gave the captain a written statement of precisely what had transpired that day.

Later that evening, some crew members left the ship to go home to their families for the night. A search party was set up at the gangway to search all bags and containers leaving the ship. The captain happened to be in attendance with Dino and another officer when Jacques arrived with what appeared to be a sack of grain on his shoulder.

When stopped and questioned, he explained that it was a sack of grain missed by the handlers and left behind earlier that day, and he was taking it across to the grain store, which was directly across the dock in full sight of the captain. With that, Dino took Jacques's ivory-handled dagger out of its sheath and punched a hole in the bottom of the sack, and with that, the grain came pouring out.

"Grain, it is all right!" exclaimed Dino.

"Get on with you".

The captain watched as Jacques carried the sack across the dock to the grain store, leaving a trail of grain behind him. Jacques emerged shortly after and went on his way.

Later in the evening, the captain gathered a few officers, including Dino. They crossed to the warehouse, which was packed to the roof with hundreds of sacks of grain. The captain finally found what he was looking for—a grain trail leading to the warehouse's far corner.

They picked out the sack with the tear and spilled it out on the ground; a little grain was left in the bottom, but the rest was mixed with spices that could easily be separated later.

This was the spice just shipped from the Orient that had been stolen from the ship's store. When spilled out, the other sacks in the pile revealed the same thing: valuable merchandise to be sold on the black market.

The captain had become suspicious when he noticed that Dino went to great pains to plunge the knife into the bottom of the sack. This was an old trick, leaving pure grain in the bottom of a sack that could be checked with a knife while the rest of the sack further up contained the stolen spice. It would be more revealing to insert the blade in the middle of the sack a few times.

If the blade met resistance, it would confirm the existence of stolen property. If there were spices hidden in the sack, the knife would have the residue of the spice on the blade. Dino pleaded his innocence, trying to place the blame on Jacques and his co-conspirators. However, on being questioned, the rest of the gang were only too happy to involve Dino to save their own skins. The captain questioned Dino further as to how he knew that the missing artifact was the statue of the goddess Bastat before they had time to do a complete inventory to check what exactly had been taken and if anything else was missing before they searched Tony's Sea chest.

How could he be so sure when he told security that the Bastat Statue was missing? The goddess Bastet, who was the Goddess of ancient Egyptian religion, had two forms. She could have the shape of a lioness or a cat's head.

"What exactly did you tell security to look for? You also knew that the key was left in the sea chest. How did you know that unless you saw it for yourself?".

Dino knew there was no way out and confessed to his involvement. The stunt Dino used of punching a hole in the sack of grain to mislead the captain was the very thing that gave him away in the end. Without the trail of grain pouring out of the sack, they would never have been able to locate the stolen goods amidst the mountain of grain sacks in the warehouse. It would have been like looking for a needle in a haystack.

Tony was set free with an apology and returned to the guesthouse that night. They collected the girls and went to the alehouse to celebrate. Jacques and his gang were nowhere to be seen. The brothers wondered what would happen on board the ship the following day. Who would take over their training: was front and foremost on their mind that night?

Chapter Five

Uskok

The two brothers were restless that night, to say the least. The following morning, they got up bright and early and made their way to the ship. They were met at the gangway and brought straight to the captain's cabin, where the ship's master and first mate were waiting with the captain. Dino was nowhere to be seen. As for Jacques, he never returned to the ship for fear of being arrested. When the strong arm of the law 'La Forza' went to arrest him, he had gone underground. Crimes of theft were punished very severely, and the dreaded Palazzo Ducale in Venice was regarded as the worst prison in the republic.

However, the other two 'de Marco' brothers, Carlos and Luigi, were there bright and early, declaring their innocence. They disavowed having any part in Jacques's crime. The captain suspected they were also complicit in the theft, but considering they were excellent sailors and needed them on the rigging, he decided to take no further action for now and let them go with a warning. James and Tony learned one lesson from all this. 'The rules that applied back home in the monastery were not the same rules and expectations in the outside world.' They would have to be more careful in the future and less trusting.

The captain had decided to speed up the training for James and Tony. He appointed Marcus, a trusted, able seaman, to take Dino's place as their new mentor. He didn't like putting a man up top without the proper training, but as they were both skilled in mountain climbing, he decided they could do 'on-the-job' training.

The captain needed riggers and good men to maintain the rigging, and now that Jacques was no longer around, he was shorthanded and needed every available man up top. Working on the rigging was one of the most important jobs, as well as being one of the most dangerous, climbing the shroud lines up to the yards and standing on foot-ropes fifty feet above the deck, often in their bare feet for fear of slipping on wet foot-ropes. Their job was furling and reefing the sails to match the ship's speed to the strength of the wind.

It could be hazardous, especially in the dark, whether on a stormy night or in the thick of battle. Falls were usually fatal whether a body hit the deck or fell into the water and drowned. The captain stressed that if either of them had any reservations or thought they were not up to the task, he would understand and make other arrangements. James and Tony were excited to finally get their own stretch of sail to manage and maintain. They promptly advised the captain that they were both ready for this opportunity and were not going to let him down.

The captain said they would sail for Sicily with the tide if the wind was favorable. He was pleased with the new arrangement and wished them both well and let them get back to work.

They spent the rest of the day with Marcus, who was an excellent climber himself. By the end of the day, they both had perfected the skill of rolling the sail and securing it to the yard or shortening the sail to compensate for the strength of the wind. They got used to the foot-rope and moved around the rigging with confidence. They would now be able to manage the sail with their eyes shut.

They were so at ease high up on the mast that they felt like they were back home on the mountain's rock face. Early the next day, before daybreak, the ship's pilot came up on deck and started yelling orders. Marcus was up there with them all the way. They were trimming and casting sails, tying up sails; they were all over that rigging like monkeys in the forest canopy.

The anchor chain was raised, and suddenly, the wind caught the sail, and the ship started to move slowly out of the lagoon and into the open sea. The sun had just peeped over the mountains, and a strong northwesterly filled the sails. They were doing two to three knots out of Venice and down into the Adriatic Sea, keeping a close eye on the coastline, making sure not to get too close to the jagged rocky shore.

The one thing they feared more than the rocky shoreline was an 'Uskok' attack. The Uskoks were Christian refugees driven out of their lands in Bosnia by Ottoman aggressors. They operated out of 'Senj,' a fortified harbor stronghold, protected by forests and mountains on land to the east and by the shallow waters to the west where the larger Venetian and

Ottoman Turkish galleys would not dare to go for fear of getting their keel stuck on the rocks.

The Uskoks had the protection of the Habsburg Emperor Ferdinand 1 of Austria, who paid them a subsidy for protecting Austria's southern border from the Ottoman Turks. Ferdinand was all too well aware of the Uskok raids on Venetian and other Mediterranean ships. It was reported that Uskok spoils of silk and jewelry finished up in the Austrian court of Ferdinand.

Although the Uskoks nominally accepted Ferdinand's sovereignty, they were a law unto themselves. They would attack in large numbers with small, fast row boats. Each boat held no more than fifty men. Their boats were powered by oars, which meant they did not depend on the tide or wind, making them more maneuverable and faster.

They would board a ship using grappling hooks and ropes. They could carry out lightning attacks and vanish just as quickly into the swamps and shallow rivers along the coastline. As well as robbing valuables, a more lucrative prize was slaves held for ransom or sold to the highest bidder on the eastern slave markets.

Over the years, the Venetian navy tried unsuccessfully to provide protection to the merchant ships sailing in and out of Venice.

On this particular morning, there was a quick change in the weather, and a mist drifted out from the coast. It was then they noticed some activity on the shore, which gradually developed into a full-scale attack by the Uskok. There were ten to fifteen of their smaller swifter boats. They were downwind of the 'Balanzara,' which was closing fast and heading straight for them. It was impossible to turn back and run. They would have to fight it out despite being completely outnumbered. Muskets and ammunition were distributed to the crew.

James and Tony stepped forward and received their weapons. Luigi de Marco joked, "Don't shoot yourself in the foot with that," directing his comment to James.

James quickly took his gun, carefully loaded the gunpowder from his powder flask, rammed his ball and wad down the barrel and patted it down until it was snug with the breech, then primed the weapon and pulled back the cock all in the space of twenty seconds.

He quickly checked the direction of the wind, made a slight correction to the sights, and pointed the gun at a seagull perched on the top of the main mast. After he shot the seagull, the white feathers fell like a winter snow flurry.

The crew acknowledged the shot with a cheer, and James looked at Luigi and said, "Now it's your turn," but Luigi replied, "How can I when you have scared all the seagulls away? It's a pity we are not fighting seagulls instead of Pirates."

The sharpshooters took up their position along each side of the ship. Cannons were filled with chains, placed on the ship's forecastle and aftercastle, and pointed at the decks in between, where the Uskok pirates were most likely to board the ship. James and Tony tried to hide their fear.

This was their first exposure to battle. They had never killed another human being. On seeing they were new to battle, the captain suggested they take up positions in the crow's nest, where they would have a good view of all that was going on down below. The captain was now on the forecastle, and his pilot was shouting commands to set all sails at full mast. The morning breeze had strengthened and was now building into a gale-force wind. James wondered what the captain was trying to do.

The 'Balanzara' was increasing its speed and closing fast on a collision course with the Uskok flotilla. Then he realized that the captain was going to ram the enemy long boats. The 'Balanzara' was strong enough; its hull was well built of solid oak, and the extra force of the wind would give the momentum needed to run the gauntlet of Uskok attackers successfully.

The Balanzara smashed into the lighter, long boats of the Uskok, creating havoc and confusion among the pirates. The attackers were taken by surprise and scattered to avoid being destroyed altogether. They were so disoriented that they lost their focus and were unable to resume their attack. The ship suffered a lot of damage and was taking on water as it kept plowing through the surf and the Uskok boats.

However, they did not have the speed to outrun all of the attackers, and even though enough damage had been done to discourage most of them, a sizable group managed to board the ship.

However, the sharpshooters quickly overcame them, each getting off an average of four shots every minute. James and Tony were creating their own havoc from the crow's nest. Tony was loading and priming the muskets, and James was finding their target. During the battle, James kept a watchful eye on the 'de Marco' brothers, Carlos and Luigi, ensuring they did not get caught in their crossfire.

During the battle, the captain took a shot to the arm and had to be taken below deck for medical attention. In his absence, the first mate took command, and the crew stood fast under increasing pressure from the pirates.

There were a few casualties among the crew, but they seemed to be getting the upper hand when two Venetian Navy ships came sailing through the mist with the wind at their back, and they were closing in fast. They fired a few warning shots that spooked the Uskok, who broke off their attack, leaving many of their own men behind to be rounded up as hostages or held for ransom and prisoner exchange.

Those that could scurry away dragged their wounded with them and headed for the shallow water of the coast, but not before the cannons fired their load with deadly effect. The ship's crew gave out a loud cheer as the navy ships arrived and took charge of the situation, taking the prisoners into custody.

The captain came back on deck to give well-deserved praise for a job well done and opened out extra rations of wine. For the first time, James and Tony felt they were accepted as members of the crew who rallied around to comment on their shooting skills—all except the 'de Marco' brothers, who blamed them for informing on their brother Jacques.

At long last, they had earned the crew's respect but knew that Carlos and Luigi would not rest until they had their revenge. The navy ships escorted the 'Balanzara' past the Uskok stronghold. They offered to escort the ship all the way to Sicily, but the captain, having assessed the damage, decided the ship, although severely damaged and letting in water, was still sea-worthy.

It was all hands to the bilge pumps as she dropped sail and headed for Sicily at a steady two knots with a south-easterly breeze at her back. The crew wasted no time clearing the deck and providing medical care for the injured. Crew members who did not survive the attack were respectfully buried at sea. The enemy bodies were disposed of similarly but without the pomp and ceremony.

Most of the damage was caused to the cargo and provisions when they were thrown about when the ship rammed the Uskok long boats.

Many of the barrels were burst open, and the contents spoiled or damaged. The biggest worry the captain had was the hull itself.

It had taken a hard knock, and many boards needed repairing and resealing with tar.

Chapter Six

Sicily

Early in the morning, with the sun still below the horizon and a cool breeze filling her sail, the 'Balanzara' with her weary crew limped into the port of Messina on the north coast of Sicily. The harbor was bustling for this time in the morning. A line of ships was waiting to get a space along the dock to unload their cargo. Many Spanish soldiers were marching here and there in small groups, and the sailors were busy milling about loading and unloading the ships.

Two Spanish warships were flying the 'St Andrew's Cross' of the Spanish navy. Philip II of the House of Hapsburg was the sovereign ruler of Spain and most of Europe, including Spain, Portugal, Italy, France, Sardinia, and Sicily. When the 'Balanzara' finally got a docking spot, the grain cargo was unloaded.

The grain had been stored in the hold of the ship, and as a result of the water damage to the lower deck, some of the grain had to be spread out on the ground to dry. Supplies and food damaged by the seawater had to be disposed of. It would take a few weeks of hard work to get the ship back in shape as a result of the Uskok attack. The ship was inspected from bow to stern, interior and exterior, and from the hull to the mast. What could not be repaired had to be replaced.

The 'Balanzara' clash with the Uskok flotilla of longboats had severely weakened the hull structure, and most of the strakes were loose and letting in water. The ship had to be careened to gain access to the hull to seal, re-caulk, and apply tar to the seams. Damaged boards needed to be replaced. The same repairs were applied to the deck to keep the water from seeping down to the lower levels.

All decks had to be cleared and swabbed. Scrubbing the decks was important for cleanliness and hygiene as disease was common on-board ships. Scrubbing was also important to preserve the wood as the saltwater would soak and swell the timber to help waterproof the deck. Gaps in the deck were packed with 'oakum' fibers made from unraveling old tarry ropes. The whole deck was finally tarred to seal it.

James and Tony were riggers, and as such, they were primarily concerned with the sails. Sails got damaged for several reasons. There was the normal wear and tear from the everyday travel, with the wind flapping against and battering the canvas sail at up to 70 mph on the ship traveling from 60 to 100 nautical miles per day.

Then there was the damage caused by stormy weather and gale force winds or in battle by cannon bombardment, both of which could be catastrophic. Sails that could not be patched or mended had to be replaced. Shrouds, ropes, yards, and masts may also need to be replaced. There were two sail-makers on board. They would cut out the patches, and James and

Tony would help sew them on. Sailors would carry a sewing kit for sail repair as part of their personal belongings.

The repair kit consisted of a seaming palm to protect their hand, needles and waxed thread and an awl for punching holes in the canvas. Guns and ammunition were continuously checked and secured. Cannon had to be tied down, and gunpowder had to be kept safe and dry.

A big part of a sailor's work on board ship was the loading and unloading of cargo along with the storing of food and provisions, together with other necessary supplies such as buckets and brooms for swabbing the deck, firewood for the galley as well as pots and pans and anything else needed for the voyage.

During a voyage, there were always food losses from spoilage or barrels not properly sealed. Water was often contaminated and had to be boiled or replaced by beer or wine. Fresh meat and vegetables had to be eaten fast before they went off. Butter would turn rancid with time; beer would go sour, and the biscuits would be reduced to dust by weevils.

After six weeks without fresh fruit and vegetables, the first signs of scurvy would start to appear from a vitamin C deficiency among the crew, with swelling of the gums and loosening of the teeth followed by lethargy and sometimes even death. Most ships would always provide a barrel of apples on deck for the crew for this reason. Apart from the health considerations, fresh food was relished on board the ship. Life and work on board a vessel was brutal and demanding for the crew, working long hours in all kinds of weather. The one thing sailors savored above all else was their grub and wine. Working men on a sailing ship need to be well-fed if the ship was to perform at its best. There were strict regulations and daily rations that each man was entitled to by law.

- 1 lb. of Hard Tack biscuit.

- ¼ lb. of cheese

- 2 oz. butter

- 1 gal. Beer/Wine

- Fresh fruit and vegetables (as needed)

- 2 lbs. salted bacon/week.

- 4 lbs. salted/pickled beef/ week

- Salted fish (usually cod) or oatmeal or rice

- Beans and/or peas.

- 1 gal. of water per month or

- 2 pints of Madeira wine mixed with 6 pints of water

- ½ pint of brandy or rum a day

Having worked feverishly for the last few days in the hot sun, the crew was eager to get ashore and have a nice cold beer to quench their thirst. It was late in the evening, and the light was beginning to fade. A group, including James and Tony, went to a local inn close by. It felt good to stand on solid ground after their ordeal with the Uskok. They ordered a few beers and sat in a quiet corner of the pub.

Despite the presence of many Spanish soldiers, the brothers felt quite at home as the voices of all the Italian sailors seemed to drown out the rest. Marcus had warned them of the dangers that lurked on the waterfront. He told them to avoid trouble and not to go anywhere alone, especially after dark. He told them to stay within their own group of friends and companions and, above all, 'to trust no one and be extra cautious of beautiful young women.'

He then told them of his own experience as a young sailor on his first visit to Sicily. He was having a quiet drink in a dockside eatery when a pretty young lady joined him. He got a little drunk, and this young lady convinced him to go for a walk along the dock and get some fresh air to sober up.

When he woke up, he found himself chained to an oar on a Barbary Coast Pirate ship. It was six months later before a Spanish warship in the West Indies rescued him. He counted himself one of the lucky ones as he worked his way back to Venice.

The harbor front was a dangerous place at night for the unsuspecting sailor. If the Venetian merchant ships were continually harassed by the Turks and the Uskok in the Adriatic, Spanish ships were constantly under attack from the Barbary Coast Pirates, especially those ships carrying treasure from the Americas. The pirates relied on oar-driven ships for speed and mobility, surprise attacks, and close hand-to-hand fighting rather than cannon. They were constantly looking for sailors to row their boats and used whatever means they could to coerce sailors to join their crews.

One tactic they used was to arrange for an alehouse landlord to advance credit for a drink to sailors down on their luck, and at the end of the night, it was a matter of pay up or work the debt off at sea. Many sailors would wake up with a hangover on a ship in the middle of the ocean, not knowing where they were or how they got there. James and Tony were well aware of the dangers as they sat quietly enjoying their drinks.

The inn was crowded with sailors and soldiers making a lot of noise. Suddenly, for a split second, Tony thought he spotted Jacques in the crowd. It was the green jacket he had often seen him wear that caught his attention. One minute, he was there; the next, he was gone. They all reassured him that Jacques was far away, somewhere behind bars.

Tony got up to take a closer look; he was so sure! But how could that be? He was checking out face after face as he looked all around the alehouse, then suddenly, he caught a fleeting glance of the green jacket again as he saw someone leave through the side door.

He followed cautiously out into the back alleyway. The alley was deserted, with no sign of anybody. It was hard to see in the fading light. He was about to give up and return inside when suddenly, out of the shadows, came a blow from behind that left him dazed and half unconscious on the ground.

Then he felt a torrent of blows to the head and kicks to the body. All he could do was curl up, using his arms to protect himself. When James and his companions came through the door to check on Tony, the attackers ran off, fleeing for their lives. James stopped for a moment and, seeing that Tony was being taken care of, continued pursuing the two attackers. They outran him, but he kept them in sight until he finally watched them board a merchant ship, the 'Brod Martolosi.'

As James walked back to Tony, he noticed something sticking up in the dirt. He instantly knew what it was when he picked it up. It was Jacques's dagger with the ivory handle. He must have dropped it in the attack. When they returned to the ship, they reported the incident to the captain and showed him the dagger they found.

The merchant ship 'Brod Martolosi' was under the command of 'Luka Ivanov Kinkovic' and based out of 'The Republic of Ragusa'. It so happened that Ragusa was a busy trading center in the Adriatic that was frequented by the 'Balanzara,' and the captains of both ships were well-known to each other. James and Captain Donai of the 'Balanzara' were in Captain Kinkovic's cabin early the following morning with the dagger as evidence.

Jacques was there all right, but he protested his innocence, claiming that his dagger was stolen and the whole thing was a case of mistaken identity. No one believed Jacques's story, but with all the crime and muggings that took place every night on the dock, it was doubtful they could make the charge of the mugging stick without definite proof, which they did not have.

However, there was still the matter of the cargo he stole from the 'Balanzara.' Jacques had been avoiding the police and was running free despite confessions from Dino and other members of the crew. Jacques could not lie his way out of this one and was escorted to a cell below deck. They say he eventually got a trip back east on a slave ship. They did not expect to hear from Jacques again, not for a very long time.

There were Spanish soldiers everywhere, not just strolling about enjoying the scenery but moving in marching units as if on a mission. Some ships were prevented from leaving the harbor. Everybody wondered if the harbor was in danger of an attack. The bigger question was by whom and for what purpose. The ship's officers spent a lot of time in the captain's cabin behind closed doors. They were very tight-lipped about whatever was being discussed.

Over the next few days, there was much speculation and anticipation that something big was coming down the pipe. Finally, the Viceroy of Sicily had a seizure notice pinned to the main mast, saying the ship was being commandeered by the Navy under the authority of Phillip II of Spain. The word on the grapevine was they were taking the ship to Dunkirk in Flanders and from there to London, England. The captain had been reassured that the seizure was for a limited period to assist with transporting soldiers and supplies to England.

The whole operation should take no more than a few weeks, after which time the ship would be returned. James and Tony wondered how all of this affected them personally. In any case, they would have to wait for further instructions from the captain. Within hours, the captain and his officers came on deck to address the crew.

The captain protested; he disagreed with his ship's takeover. He had personally sent notice of his disapproval to the highest authority. This was a Venetian ship of the Sovereign Republic of Venice, and any such seizure would be regarded as an act of war.

However, his superiors back in Venice had overruled him for political expediency. They did not want to oppose the takeover and upset the Hapsburg Emperor in Austria, which bordered the Republic of Venice.

Sailors had the choice to return to Venice, or they were welcome to stay with the ship and be well paid for their service. The mission was simple! To transport soldiers and supplies to the English Channel and escort a Spanish army under the command of the Duke of Parma from Flanders to the English coast.

As they had more firepower than the English and a much superior fighting force, there was nothing to be concerned about. James and Tony figured it would only be a matter of weeks before they would be back in the arms of Maria and Rosa. They saw this as an opportunity to broaden their shipping experience in the Atlantic and also because they wanted to stay with the ship that they saw as key to their future success.

Needless to say, Marcus did not take the Viceroy up on his offer. Having said goodbye to James and Tony, he took the next ship back to Venice. He promised to convey their apologies to Maria and Rosa as they would be a few weeks late in getting back to Venice, and he would also let Michael Simone know what had happened to their ship in Sicily.

James and Tony were well aware of King Philip's connection with the English Crown. They read of King Henry's marriage to Catherine of Aragon, Catherine's catholic daughter Mary's succession to the English throne, and her marriage to Philip of Spain. With the rise of Protestantism in England, how Mary persecuted the protestant reformists. She was better known as 'Bloody Mary'.

After her death, leaving no heir, Mary had thought that she would be succeeded by Mary Queen of Scotts, the granddaughter of Henry's sister

Eileen. However, she was succeeded by her half-sister Elizabeth, the protestant daughter of Henry and Ann Boleyn.

The 'Act of Uniformity' made Protestantism the official religion in England, and 'The Act of Supremacy' made Elizabeth the supreme governor of the Church of England. That same year, Elizabeth turned down a proposal from Philip of Spain. Elizabeth signed the Treaty of Nonsuch, where she promised military support for the Dutch rebel revolt against the rule of Philip II of Spain, an action that constituted an undeclared act of war.

Phillip was also upset at Elizabeth's privateers who attacked Spanish settlements and cities in the New World and her Sea Dog pirates who, under the leadership of Sir Francis Drake, raided Spanish ships laden with treasure on the high seas.

Phillip's initial plan was to invade England with an army under the command of the Marquis of Santa Cruz. The plan was to escort Santa Cruz and his army across the English Channel, incite the English Catholics to rebel, and join his forces to install Mary Queen of Scotts, a Catholic, on the English throne. However, in the meantime, Elizabeth ordered the execution of her half-sister Mary.

This prompted Phillip's decision to take the English throne for himself. Phillip decided to use his own army, which was currently fighting rebels in Holland under the command of one of the best military soldiers at the time, the Duke of Parma. When his supreme commander, Santa Cruz, died suddenly, Philip was forced to choose the less qualified Duke of Medina Sidonia as the new supreme commander of his fleet.

Sidonia's orders were to sail up the English Channel and meet up with Parma's army, which would be waiting in Flanders, and escort them in a flotilla of barges across the channel, where both of them were to join forces and lay siege to London.

Chapter Seven
The Trinidad Valencera

Philip of Spain had assembled a massive fleet of 132 ships to transport his army of 30,000 soldiers to invade England under the command of the Duke of Sidonia. They would be joined by an additional 30,000 soldiers, currently fighting the Dutch in Flanders, under the command of the Duke of Parma. Philip had spent over 10 million ducats on ammunition, military equipment, uniforms, and six months' food supply and provisions to feed his army. He was finally ready to put his plan into action, to invade England and take over the throne from Elizabeth.

All of the men and provisions were packed into the already overcrowded ships. The logistics of this plan were enormous and prone to disaster from the start. The 'Balanzara' and its Venetian captain 'Horatio Donai' were placed under Spanish captain Don Alonzo de Luzon's command. The ship was refitted to transport an additional 281 Spanish soldiers, weapons, supplies, and equipment together with the usual crew of 79 and a cadre of officers.

She was renamed the 'Trinidad Valencera' and fitted with 42 cannons. The cargo also included three large 40-pound siege cannon that was donated by Philip 11 of Spain and designed by the famous Belgian Gunsmith "Remigy de Halut."

The deck was packed with explosives of all kinds that included additional barrels of gunpowder and ammunition for the invasion. They also carried a large consignment of 'bomba ceramic fire pots' packed with flammable material to be thrown among the sails of enemy ships. Usually, the only people apart from the officers allowed on the upper deck were those defending the ship and the crew, including the riggers, repairing and maintaining the sails, and scrubbing the decks.

All other soldiers and sailors were billeted and confined to the lower decks. On this voyage, however, every inch of space available was used. Soldiers and supplies were everywhere, getting in the way of those trying to do their jobs and slowing everybody down.

The stockpile of explosives on deck and the overcrowding posed a real hazard to the ship and the crew. James and Tony were aware of the situation, and while they were not happy with the impending danger, they were comforted in the knowledge that it would all be over soon, a few weeks at most, and when they finally delivered their cargo of men and supplies, they would be on their way back home.

James and Tony stayed on board the ship for long hours each day. Most of the time, they spent checking the sails and the food supplies. They would also keep themselves busy patching the canvas sails, tying up ropes, checking that all the blocks and tackles were working properly, and testing rope ladders. There was always plenty to do on a ship as big as the 'Trinidad

Valencera.' Everyone was busy making sure the ship was totally sea-worthy.

Shipwrights, carpenters, pitch smelters, coopers, and blacksmiths were below deck, carrying out maintenance and repairs to the hull to ensure the ship was watertight. Every repair was carefully and painstakingly carried out as a precaution to ensure the smooth, trouble-free operation of the ship. In the middle of a storm or during an enemy attack, there would be no time for checking the rigging or carrying out routine maintenance and repair.

They would check and recheck every halyard, brace, sheet, and shroud; a problem with any one of them in the thick of battle or stormy weather could spell disaster for them all. Everything had to be ship-shape to ensure the safety of the sailors and crew, especially those working high up on the rigging in all types of weather.

The 'Trinidad Valencera' was built as a merchant ship to carry grain and cargo from one port to another, and despite its sturdy design, it was not a warship that required a much more solid construction. The constant discharge and recoil of forty-two cannons would put a heavy strain on the structure of a merchant ship. It was never expected that the 'Trinidad Valencera' would be drawn into a full-scale battle with the enemy.

The regular Spanish warships were there to take on the heavy fighting. The accepted modus operandi of attack for the Spanish fleet was to fire one decisive salvo at the enemy, follow up with close musket fire, and finally board the enemy ship with superior forces. Cannon was not something the 'Trinidad Valencera' was particularly suited for, as a means of defense, maybe! as a means of attack, not so much. Each cannon required an additional crew of four men and had to be tightly lashed down to the deck so they would not fly about when fired, causing damage to the ship and injury to the crew. The last thing you wanted was a loose cannon on an overcrowded deck.

The English had known for many months that the Spanish were preparing for war. It was not possible to keep a secret of that magnitude for long. A few months earlier, in April of that year, Sir Francis Drake attacked a small fleet of Spanish ships at Cadiz on the Spanish coast: Sir Francis Drake was the first English man to circumnavigate the world and only the third overall. A privateer commissioned by Queen Elizabeth I and branded a pirate by Philip II of Spain, who is said to have offered six million pounds for his capture, dead or alive.

He had attacked and looted many Spanish treasure ships and settlements in the West Indies. Drake and his cousin John Hawkins were also slave traders who transported slaves from Africa and sold them to settlers in the Viceroyalty of New Spain. Queen Elizabeth awarded him a knighthood for his achievements and service to the Crown.

He was now the vice-admiral of the English fleet. Drake, with twenty-six vessels under his command and two Dutch ships, made a surprise attack on the Spanish ships anchored at Cadiz. The attack was carried out under a veil of secrecy. None of the ships flew a flag or had any identifying banners. There were spies everywhere on both sides, so secrecy was paramount. Misleading information was sent to the English ambassador in Paris, who was suspected to be in the pay of the Spanish. A last-minute communication was issued by the queen, 'not to engage the Spanish,' whether that message was a deceptive hoax to deceive the Spanish or a genuine message that arrived too late, we will never know.

They entered the bay of Cadiz at dusk, catching the Spanish fleet off guard. During the ensuing battle, they encountered heavy fire from the shore defenses, but not before they burned and destroyed over 24 of the Spanish ships and looted or destroyed over ten thousand tons of supplies and equipment. Drake and his fleet continued to raid and loot ships and ports all along the Iberian coast on their way back to England.

The raid, with the loss of ships and equipment, put Philip's plan to invade England back at least three or four months. It meant additional food supplies and provisions were needed to replace those destroyed. A bigger problem was the fact that some provisions already delivered were already nearing their shelf life, and any further delay could have serious consequences. Large quantities of staves used to make barrels for storing food were seized in the raid on Cadiz, resulting in a shortage of barrels to store food.

The raid on Cadiz did not stop Philip's plan to invade England and was referred to as 'a singeing of the King of Spain's beard', playing down the seriousness of the attack, but if the truth be known, it put a severe strain on the supply of food and provisions and the barrels to store it.

As it was, suppliers were hard-pressed to fill the original orders to feed Philip's vast army, and in many cases, the quality and freshness were less than satisfactory. The only saving grace, in the opinion of James and Tony, was the expectation of a short voyage, there and back, but this gave little solace to the quartermaster. However, provisions would have to be carefully monitored and supervised. Secrecy was maintained at every level. Passing information unwittingly or otherwise was severely punished. There were spies everywhere, and everyone was treated with suspicion.

The raid on Cadiz was blamed on loose talk among the sailors. As they say, 'loose lips sink ships.' While this delay did not stop the invasion, it gave the English more time to upgrade and reinforce their crumbling defenses, which were considered old, out of date, and not likely to withstand attacks from an invading army.

It also gave them time to set up fire beacons all along the south coast as an early warning signal to London of the Spanish arrival. A militia was set up to defend the queen in London. New battle strategies were developed that relied more on heavy cannon fire, speed and maneuverability, and less hand-to-hand fighting that favored the Spanish.

On the 'Trinidad Valencera,' not only were the decks overcrowded with soldiers and crew, but the ship also carried animals that included horses, mules, cows, and chickens. The animals would provide fresh meat, milk, cheese, and eggs. With so many people and animals crowded together in a confined space, conditions on board were extremely unpleasant, noisy, smelly, filthy, and a health hazard, a perfect breeding ground for disease. The most common illness on board a ship was Dysentery or 'bloody flux' as it was more commonly called. Typhoid with outbreaks of Salmonella were also common.

The symptoms included fever, abdominal pain, constipation, and dehydration. They were usually caused by the contamination of food and the water supply. Proper storage and hygiene in preparing and serving food were critical for a healthy crew. Poor sanitation often gave rise to cholera. Smallpox was feared as the deadliest and most painful disease of all. Thousands of sailors die from this disease each year. Lice was also a problem on overcrowded ships.

The most important job on board the ship was the scrubbing of the deck, which had to be carried out daily and more often if needed. The deck had to be kept clean, and the bilge pumps emptied as often as possible. It was impossible to get rid of the smell of vomit and human feces. The beakhead at the bow of the ship was equipped with toilet seats of ease and a grated floor that allowed the seawater to wash away the filth and vomit and reduce the smell.

The galley was located in the middle of the ship, as far away as possible from the powder magazine and explosives. Special care was always required in preparing, storing, and distributing food. It was normal for the crew to collect their rations themselves and find a place to sit and eat. However, with the extra people to feed on this voyage, it was more convenient to distribute the rations at stations located on each level. Food and rations were delivered to the sick by the younger sailors. James and Tony were assigned to assist the purser and the quartermaster and help oversee the distribution of food on the ship as part of their duties.

By the middle of May, the Fleet was ready to set sail from Lisbon, flying the 'Armada Flag' specially designed for the invasion of England and was flown on all Spanish ships, including the 'Trinidad Valencera.' The flag design included The Crest of Imperial Spain, surrounded by a blue band on a field of white. It had been blessed by Pope Pius V in support of the invasion.

The fleet had been anchored along the Tagus River, waiting for a favorable wind. Initially, the wind from the north forced the bigger ships to drift south, but by mid-June, they finally got a southwesterly to set them back on course. James and Tony could not hide their excitement when they took their place in the fleet formation of 130 ships of all shapes and sizes in the middle of the Atlantic Ocean, ready to set sail for the English Channel. As they neared the Bay of Biscay, the wind started to strengthen, and before long, they found themselves in gale-force winds.

The Bay of Biscay was notorious for its bad weather, and as the storm strengthened, it turned into a hurricane with hundred-mile-and-hour gale-force winds. James and Tony were furling and tying up the sails on the main mast. The strong winds caught many of the crew by surprise, tearing sails to shreds, shattering yards and bards, and sending debris flying in every direction—the crowded decks of soldiers cowering for protection. The strong winds were testing the strength and the preparedness of the fleet. Sails had to be trimmed back and rolled up for safety. The storm lasted for three days.

When the weather eased, it was possible to get a clear assessment of the overall damage. The decks were cleared and scrubbed, and everything was put away securely. The hull and the rigging were inspected for damage. Much of the damage could not be fixed at sea, and the fleet was forced to put in for repairs and shelter at 'A Coruna' in northern Spain.

In one way, this storm was probably the best thing that could happen; if anything were to go wrong, this was the time. Most of the soldiers on board were beginning to get seasick and were hanging over the edge. There were a lot of injuries among the men. Most of the injuries were minor, but there were a few severe concussions where crew members were struck by falling debris. Thankfully, there were no fatal injuries.

Some of the food was spoiled in the storm. Barrels containing fresh water and provisions had been knocked about and damaged. James and

Tony set about making a detailed inspection to assess the extent of the damage. This allowed the brothers to get to know their way around the food storage. They secured every remaining barrel with ropes and made a detailed inventory of all food supplies. Once they reached their destination, made landfall, and unloaded their cargo of military men and supplies, they would be in a better position to see what was needed.

They could then put into any port on their way back to Spain and replenish their food supplies. There was no real cause for concern if everything else went according to plan. James and Tony were kept busy repairing and replacing sails, securing foot ropes, and working on the rigging. Whenever they got a chance, they helped the medics with those injured by falling debris.

The first aid they learned on the mountain rescue expeditions back home at the monastery proved useful. The medics were stretched to their limit, and any help they got was welcome. There were sick and wounded everywhere, and the stench of vomit filled the air. There was barely room to move on the overcrowded deck.

When James and Tony were not helping with the sick and injured, they liked to spend as much time as possible high up on the rigging where they could breathe the clean, fresh sea air and get away from the smell that lingered no matter how often the deck was scrubbed. The fleet spent the next few weeks in port repairing the damage caused by the storm and taking on fresh supplies. Five ships in all had to abandon the trip and turn back, four galleys and one galleon, leaving 128 ships to continue on to the English Channel.

By mid-July, it was every man to his post. The anchors were raised, sails were billowing in the wind, and sailors were climbing the rope ladders, unraveling sails, and tying ropes. The fleet of 128 ships set sail for the English Channel under the command of the Duke of Medina-Sidonia on the 'Sao Martinho,' the flagship of the commander and chief. Sidonia was an aristocrat without naval command experience. He was neither a soldier nor a sailor.

He was selected by Philip II himself, who knew that there were plenty of other commanders with lots of experience to assist Sidonia, but it was yet to be seen if he had the experience needed to evaluate and take their advice.

The Spanish Fleet was divided into ten separate squadrons. The 'Trinidad Valencera' was one of ten ships in the Christian 'Levant' squadron under the command of 'Martin de Burtendona on his flagship, the 'La Regazona.' The captain of the 'Trinidad Valencera' was Don Alonzo de Luzon.'

Philip had been preparing for three years, and now, despite some setbacks, his fleet was ready to sail for Flanders. It took two days for all the ships to clear the harbor. The remaining 128 Ships, 8000 Sailors, 18000 soldiers, and 2500 canons set sail for Flanders.

Chapter Eight
Gravelines

By mid-July of that year, the Spanish fleet was spotted off the south coast of England. Signal fires were set ablaze as a warning beacon that lit up the night sky all the way to London to alert their arrival. James saw the beacon as a sign they had finally reached the English Coast and would soon be returning to Spain and, from there, home to Venice, to Maria and Rosa.

The English fleet did not expect the Spanish so soon and were still anchored in Plymouth Harbor. The Spanish scouts reported they were trapped there and waiting for the wind to change in their favor. The great drawback with sailing ships was they relied completely on the wind and the tide for mobility. Smaller boats could be driven by oars or a combination of oars and sail. The English fleet, which was mostly sail, was trapped helplessly in Plymouth.

This presented an opportunity for Sidonia, the Spanish commander, to attack and destroy the English fleet. Aboard the 'Trinidad Valencera,' the order went out to prepare to engage the enemy. It was all hands to their stations. The cannons were ready and loaded; the sharpshooters took up vantage positions along the deck, and high up on the forecastle, boarding parties were ready to go at a moment's notice.

However, at the last minute, Philip ordered Sidonia to call off the attack and proceed without delay to Flanders, as initially planned, to pick up Parma's army in their flotilla of barges and escort them across the channel to England. James and Tony were relieved by this change of plan; they were sailors and not soldiers, and they did not want to be caught up in a war in a foreign country by an emperor to whom they owed no allegiance. This was not their fight, a war they had been forced into. The way they saw it, the sooner they could deliver their cargo and get to hell back home, the better.

Eventually, the tide changed in favor of the English, and fifty-five ships set out from Plymouth to engage the Spanish fleet. The English split up into two groups: one group of twelve ships led by Sir Francis Drake tacked to the north along the Cornish coast, upwind of the Spanish, while the other larger group sailed south.

They could now attack the Spanish from two different directions. The English sailors were completely overawed by the sheer scale of the Spanish fleet, one hundred and twenty-eight ships in a quarter moon defensive crescent formation, with its convex to the east.

The larger ships, including the 'Trinidad Valencera,' took up their positions in the middle and at each end of the pincher formation, where they could close in on any intruder attacking the smaller cargo ships in the center.

The English ships were much smaller, faster, and more maneuverable than the Spanish. They were longer and could accommodate more cannon along their flank. Their cannons were smaller, easier to handle, and faster to reload.

The Spanish ships were higher, with castles front and rear. This gave them the height advantage when boarding enemy ships as they favored close hand-to-hand fighting. The English had a completely different strategy. They preferred to keep their distance and avoid close-up 'man-to-man' fighting.

They relied solely on cannon fire at a safe distance, so they didn't have any combat soldiers on board their ships. The English were extremely cautious not to get too close to the Spanish fleet, using their speed and rapid-fire power to inflict a devastating assault at a safe distance. They could fire a ten to twenty-pound cannonball up to twelve hundred feet. The one big advantage the English had was their maneuverability. They had mastered the art of sailing against the wind. A system known as tacking or sailing close to the wind.

They could zig-zag diagonally across the wind while achieving a forward motion overall. This maneuver allowed Drake's fleet to get behind the Spanish with the wind at his back. As long as the English ships had the weather gauge, they were in complete control, as the Spanish could not pursue them against the wind. This was very confusing to James, who watched from his vantage point high up in the ship's main mast.

He could see the fleet stretched out on either side and the smaller English ships coming in close, firing their cannon and moving away fast, out of range of the bigger Spanish ships. The Spanish had to rely on their cannon fire more than they intended. Their cannon was bigger and more complex to reload, especially on a crowded deck. The standard battle tactics of the Spanish forces was to bombard the enemy first with cannon fire, followed by the sharpshooters at close quarters, and finally to board and overpower the enemy vessel with sheer numbers, a tried and tested plan of attack used in the Mediterranean in the battle of Lepanto against the Turks and overseas in the Americas. However, this tactic would not work without the weather gauge. The Spanish needed the wind in their sail to mount any attack.

The 'Trinidad Valencera' took much of the enemy fire. Such a large ship presented a sizable target even at long range. The ship took hits above and below the waterline, weakening the whole structure. While the English directed their fire mainly at the hull in an effort to damage and sink the ship, the most damage was caused to the rigging using chain, scissor, and crossbar shot in an attempt to render the ship dead in the water and at the mercy of their smaller and faster ships.

At that distance, the rigging presented the easiest target, and the continuous bombardment left some Spanish ships unable to maneuver out of harm's way. Cannonballs making a direct hit on the ship sent wooden splinters hurling across the deck, maiming sailors and, in some cases, even cutting them in half.

On some ships, gun ports ran red with blood with so many casualties on board. There was absolute panic on board amid all the turmoil and destruction caused by the English bombardment. After the shelling died down, James and Tony, who had taken cover on deck during the attack, scampered up the rigging to inspect the damage. Their rigging section was still intact, so they headed back down to help with the wounded. The ship had taken on a lot of water. Many of the barrels had been thrown about and leaked their contents, while others had let in seawater. The pumps were working nonstop to bring the flooding under control.

The carpenters and the pitch workers worked at a fever pitch to shore up the leaks. Teams of men were trying to salvage what food and supplies they could. James and Tony knew straight away that the food would have to be rationed for the rest of the voyage. James knew that when the food situation was assessed correctly, the full extent of the damage would be a lot worse than the initial inspection showed.

However, they presumed that the food situation did not present a major problem as the 'Trinidad Valencera' would be able to replenish their supplies when they reached England.

Very little else had changed between the two sides. No ships had been completely destroyed and sank in the attacks. However, two Spanish ships, the 'Nuestra Del Rosario' and the 'San Salvador,' were abandoned after they collided. Nobody was surprised when the 'San Salvador 'whose decks were loaded with ammunition exploded, lighting up the night sky and pinpointing their position. Later in the dark of night, Drake sailed out with a boarding party and looted the Rosario for badly needed supplies of gunpowder and ammunition.

When the 'San Salvador' exploded, Drake realized the big weakness in Philip's plan. The large amounts of explosives the Spanish ships were carrying presented a major hazard that the English could exploit. In the stealth of night, Drake stole back to his fleet without being noticed.

In the morning light, the English fleet used their speed and manœuvrability to regroup for a continued attack. They attempted to engage the Spanish fleet again off Portland Bill lighthouse.

However, the Spanish had the weather advantage and tried to close the gap and board the English ships, which were too fast and maneuverable for the Spanish to get within range. James, Tony, and the rest of the crew were exhausted and needed some time to rest up and reassess their situation, take a deep breath, and decide how best to get the ship back into shape. They needed a safe harbor where they could shelter while waiting for the signal from Parma's army saying they were ready to rendezvous.

The Solent Strait between the 'Isle of White' and the mainland presented the perfect solution. It was over three miles wide and 20 miles long.

However, Sidonia feared that a frontal attack by the English would drive the Spanish fleet into the shallow waters of the 'Owers shoals' at the other end of the strait.

Using an abundance of caution, he ordered his fleet back to the open sea. Three Spanish ships stayed and faced off against two English ships, the 'Ark Royal' and the 'Golden Lion. They exchanged fire for a couple of hours without any real damage to either of the ships. There was no other safe harbor on the south coast of England, leaving the Spanish with no option but to continue their course east towards Dunkirk, where they hoped Parma's army would be ready and waiting.

It was the end of July when James and Tony and the 'Trinidad Valencera' took up its position in the fleet as they anchored off Calais. It was not a safe harbor; they did not have much room to maneuver in the event of an attack, but Sidonia wanted his fleet close together in case he had to move fast. Parma finally responded to Sidonia with the bad news. He was concerned with the high incidents of mortality among his soldiers who were crammed into unhygienic and disease-ridden camps.

His army was now reduced to half because of disease and sickness and were not yet ready to move out and meet up with the fleet. He had not yet received all the barges he needed to transport what was left of his army across the channel to England. It would take another six days at least before he would be ready to move out.

However, the Dutch navy that supported Elizabeth was blockading the shallow water port of Dunkirk with thirty flyboats. The flyboat was a flat-bottomed vessel suitable for canals and rivers. Parma's barges would risk inevitable slaughter if they tried to move out without the protection of the Spanish fleet.

Parma needed Sidonia to attack the Dutch and neutralize this threat. Sidonia would not risk his bigger ships to attack the smaller, lighter Dutch ships for fear of running aground in the shallow water shoals of Flanders and Zeeland. Sidonia had also decided that because of his fleet's vulnerability and not having a safe port, he needed all of his smaller ships for his own protection until Parma was ready to move. He decided that he could not go to the aid of Parma as things now stood. The whole situation was fluid and changing by the minute. Sidonia hoped that everything would come together when Parma was ready to launch his barges.

James and Tony had time to check the damage to the food supplies. They would land in England soon and have an opportunity to take on fresh water and food, enough to get them back to Spain. They were glad of the break in the fighting. They tried to get some sleep as they did not know what problems the coming days would bring. The entire fleet was tightly packed and anchored close to each other. They were ready to move out at short notice when the orders came down.

It was around midnight when Drake finally got the opportunity to exploit the one weakness the Spanish fleet was not prepared for and did not see coming. The English loaded eight of their own ships with flammable and explosive materials. They set them alight and floated them downwind into the close formation of the Spanish defenses.

The sky was suddenly lit up, and the alarm was raised. Every man rushed to take up his position, and the cannon was loaded and made ready for the oncoming attack. It took a while before they realized the danger as the fireships continued to bear down on them. The dark sky was lit up as explosion after explosion spewed out sparks, fire, and brimstone on the tightly packed Spanish formation. Two of the fire ships were intercepted and towed away, but the other six were being carried by the wind and headed straight into the Spanish close-knit defensive positions. Many of the smaller ships that were overloaded with explosives panicked, cutting their anchor and fleeing in the midst of all the confusion to get out of the way and avoid the danger of the fire ships exploding.

As they fled the danger, they scattered and did not have the weather gauge to recover their defensive position in the crescent formation with the fleet. The bigger Spanish ships, including the 'Trinidad Valencera' and, of course, the flagships, held their position as the English followed up with a full frontal attack.

The Spanish found themselves in an untenable situation. The English were blocking the channel to the west, and Sidonia did not want to sail further east into the shallow waters off Flanders and Zeeland, where the Dutch had removed all the markers warning the larger ships of the danger. Instead, He decided to regroup and make a stand at the small port of Gravelines.

The English were well aware of the Spanish fighting strategy of boarding the enemy ship and using their greater numbers to overwhelm their enemy with pistols and cutlasses as opposed to cannon. They were also aware that the Spanish vessels were so crowded with ammunition supplies that it was not easy or safe to repeatedly continue to reload and fire their cannon in the heat of the battle.

The swifter English fleet used their superior speed and maneuverability to provoke fire while maintaining a safe distance from the Spanish cannon fire. After the Spanish fired a salvo, they could move in closer and concentrate their cannon fire more effectively at a more damaging range. The Spanish ships, which were trying to aim their cannon broadside at the English, being downwind, were forced by the strong winds to expose their healing hulls below the waterline.

At the same time, the Spanish found it impossible to aim their cannon with any accuracy while their cannon was elevated in the air as the wind forced the ship to lean backward. The English fleet inflicted devastating broadside attacks, one after another, with maximum damage to the ships and their crews.

The English ships were close enough to exchange musket fire with the Spanish but not close enough to be boarded by them. After eight hours of fighting, the English were running out of ammunition, and by 4 pm in the afternoon, the English pulled back.

Four Spanish ships had been lost, including 'The San Lorenzo,' 'The San Mateus,' 'The San Filipe,' and 'The Maria Juan'. Many of the other ships were severely damaged, especially the bigger galleons that bore the brunt of the fighting, including the 'Trinidad Valencera.'

Chapter Nine

The North Sea

The battle-weary crew of the 'Trinidad Valencera' was relieved when the English fleet retreated and fell back. She had been in the thick of the battle at Gravelines even though she had not had time to recover from earlier attacks in the week. She had held her ground against persistent bombardment from the English fleet with terrible consequences. The 'Trinidad Valencera' had taken a number of hits below the water line when her starboard bow was elevated and exposed as she struggled against the strong winds.

Water was gushing into the ship faster than it could be pumped out. As a quick repair, men had to be lowered over the side to patch the holes with lead sheeting. This stopped the water from gushing into the hold, but it was still seeping in through many seams and loose boards. The carpenters and pitchers worked tirelessly, and the bilge pumps worked nonstop to control the flooding.

The ship was barely holding together below deck, while the rigging was in tatters above deck. Her sails were shredded, and her soldiers and crew had suffered more than their fair share of casualties. The decks were crowded with injured men seeking medical help while others lay dead or wounded where they fell. The place was littered with debris, with yards, sail, and pieces of timber strewn around the deck. Splinters of wood were scattered everywhere, and many of the splinters had found their way with lethal effect into the bodies of many of the soldiers and crew. It was chaos on board the ship; there was little or no room to move on deck with all the noise and shouting.

Amidst the turmoil and panic, James and Tony, who had suffered some bruises and minor cuts, scampered up the shroud without a thought for their own safety. They and every other available body were on the rigging, patching and mending what was left of the sail. This was a fight for their very survival. There was no time to lick their wounds or take a breather. The ship needed sail, and sail it would have.

Both James and Tony were working feverishly to patch and repair what was left of the sail in their care. After a few hours and a few temporary fixes, they patched up their section of sail. It would hold, but for how long depended entirely on the weather. The overall assessment of the rigging was a lot of damage, requiring a lot of work to put it right, but for now, the ship would sail even if not very well.

The officers were trying hard to take control of the situation. They were shouting commands from the castle, and everyone relied on them for direction. Everyone was relieved as order was finally restored, and people were finally being taken care of. Bodies were checked for vital signs, and the dead were taken to one side.

The sick and dying were quickly triaged and organized as best they could with the limited medical resources available. James and Tony rushed about the deck assisting the medics, looking after the injured, cleaning and dressing wounds, and giving water and blankets to those in shock, making them as comfortable as possible and trying to ease their pain. They spent the rest of the night cleaning the deck, gathering debris, throwing it overboard, and catching a few hours of sleep along the way.

The next day, there was some talk that the fleet would regroup and sail back to Dunkirk to meet with Parma's army. The English fleet was downwind in the Channel, cutting off any return to Spain. The only way they could move was east; however, the crippled Spanish fleet was dangerously close to running aground in the sands of Zeeland. Eventually, the wind changed in their favor, and now, with the wind from the south at their back, the Spanish fleet decided to sail into the North Sea with the English in pursuit.

Having weighed their options, the Spanish joint command decided to cut off any engagement with the English and take the fleet home. On hearing that, the plan to join Parma's army was no longer viable, and the attack on London had been abandoned. This gave cold chills down the spines of James and Tony.

On the one hand, they were glad they were going home, but on the other, they wondered if the ship could make it back to Spain in its present condition. The food situation suddenly went from bad to disastrous. After Sidonia and his advisors reviewed the situation, they decided they were still active in a war situation. They wanted to avoid another battle with the English, who were now blocking the Channel to the west and their way home to Spain. The other option was to follow a very precise route around Scotland and Ireland and sail home to Spain by way of the Atlantic, but staying well clear of the coast.

The weather was fair to moderate, with a steady wind from the southeast. There was every chance that if the weather held, they could all make it home to Spain. The English were almost out of ammunition but continued to pursue the Spanish fleet up the North Sea. Sidonia surmised this was the case but would not call their bluff. His priority now was to get his crippled fleet home to Spain.

Sidonia still had 110 ships under his command, many badly damaged by cannon fire, some missing their anchors that were cut loose at Calais, all ships running short on food and water, decks full of dead, wounded, and sick soldiers, and nearly all ships letting in water. At the beginning of August, the English broke off their pursuit at the Firth of Forth off Scotland. Most of the Spanish vessels were still capable of making it back to Spain with a bit of luck and fair weather. If they could stay together, they would stand a better chance, but some were in such need of repair they started to lag behind, including the 'Trinidad Valencera.'

Sidonia planned to sail towards the coast of Norway and turn west at the northern tip of the Shetland Islands, well clear of the Scottish coast. From Shetland, they would sail west to Rockall, which is an uninhabitable massive granite rock in the North Atlantic Ocean. From Rockall Rock, it is a straight voyage directly south to Spain, staying well to the west of the Irish coastline. Unfortunately, the navigation officers were poorly trained in latitude sailing and dead reckoning.

They had no experience of these waters and made no allowance for the Gulf Stream that pushed them eastwards. Their navigational charts were not accurate. Stormy weather over Norway threw the fleet off course. They turned west too early and passed between the Orkney and Fair Islands, much closer to the Scottish coast than anticipated, and as they headed out into the Atlantic, they were pushed back towards the rocky coast of Ireland by stormy weather and the Gulf Stream.

Many of the ships were not seaworthy and difficult to handle. The crews were suffering from stress and fatigue, and the ship's decks were overcrowded with sick and injured seamen.

James and Tony tried to keep their mind on the task at hand, maintaining and repairing the sail as best they could, looking after the sick and wounded, serving food, and distributing rations to those who couldn't look after themselves. The kitchen or cook box was set up on a bed of sand and rocks below the forecastle where a sailor normally could go to get his bowl filled.

Each man on board had his own bucket and wooden bowl for his rations and wine.

Rations at this stage were hard-tack and salted pork. The first symptoms of scurvy were starting to appear: swelling of the gums and blotches on the skin. As the days passed and the food became scarce, meat began to spoil, butter turned rancid, beer and wine began to go sour, and the hardtack that wasn't destroyed by sea water was reduced to dust by the weevil. Every sailor carried a fishing line as part of his personal belongings in his sea chest, along with his other possessions of socks, Petticoats, Breeches, Jacket or Jerkin, slops, caps and shoes, wooden bowls, and buckets.

They also carried a sewing kit to repair and fashion their own clothes and an oilskin for wet weather. To avoid sleeping in wet clothes, they always carried extra. Some sailors would also have a fiddle or tin whistle to play when off duty. The music took their mind off their troubles and helped them relax.

The 'Trinidad Valencera' was fortunate to run across a fishing boat returning from the North Atlantic laden with herring from the cold shores of Greenland. Fresh fish was a welcome addition to their meager rations, for a few days at least. The fishing gear was also confiscated, but they did not expect to catch a whole lot of fish in these waters, but every little helped. Amid the turmoil, suffering, and grief on board the 'Trinidad Valencera,' despair started to set in among the crew.

They felt they were cursed with one disaster after another. Sailors believed they were in the hands of God when they were at sea. They prayed to God, the blessed virgin, and their patron saints to keep them safe. Swearing, Gambling, and Foul language were not tolerated. Even playing card games was discouraged on some ships.

To avoid any fears or superstitions, the captain decided to turn to religion to try and lift their spirits. Right now, the most pressing task was to bury the dead that were piled up on the deck, so arrangements were made for the burial service.

The captain was not aware that the pastor had sustained a serious head wound and could not carry out the burial service. In his absence, he asked if anyone would like to say a few words. Tony and James had been present at many burial services back at the monastery; however, they hesitated, not being fluent in Spanish.

On reflection, they realized the crew spoke many different languages but were all familiar with the Latin prayers common throughout the Catholic Church, especially in Spain and Italy. Tony stepped forward, and proceeded with the complete burial service in Latin, and added a few prayers of his own.

The ship's crew may not have understood the language, but they were all deeply aware and engrossed in the service's solemnity. After the service, the bodies of the dead soldiers and seamen were, one by one, committed to the deep.

The captain realized that this had a calming effect on the crew. They would always resign themselves to the will of God when their lives were threatened with danger and disaster.

It was crucial now more than ever to get the pastor back on his feet. However, as the days passed, the pastor's condition went from bad to worse. The medics confirmed that he was suffering from internal bleeding sustained by a blow to the head by flying debris and was not expected to last. It was the custom of the pastor to lead the crew in prayer each morning, followed by a service and blessing. The captain felt that this service was essential to boost the morale of the crew and should continue to provide some comfort to the men, many of whom were now dying from injury and disease on board his ship.

He spoke to Tony about taking over as pastor to the crew. While Tony was happy to help out where he could, he feared that the crew would see any attempt to replace the pastor as pretentious. To increase their standing among the men, the captain transferred both brothers to the officers' quarters. A move that did not please the 'de Marco' boys, Carlos and Luigi, who had not been seen for some time but had not forgiven James and Tony for what happened to their brother Jacques.

The captain brought Tony into his cabin and handed him a Franciscan monk's habit belonging to the pastor. He then went to a small oak chest and took out a crucifix and a rosary. The crucifix was made of solid gold and contained the relic of St. Francis of Assisi. It was inlaid with diamonds and had a gold chain. The Rosary was a work of art, beautifully designed with precious stones, reportedly to have once belonged to Queen Isabella herself.

The captain handed them to Tony and told him to wear them, saying, "If these don't impress the crew, nothing will." The following morning, Tony appeared on deck and called the crew and soldiers to prayer. He started with the 'Sign of the Cross' in Latin, '*In Nominee Patris, et Felii et Spiritus Sancti.*'

Blessing the crowd and sprinkling holy water on those present. He continued with the 'Lord's Prayer' which everybody was familiar with,

'*Pater Noster, qui es in caelis, sanctificetur nomen tuum. Fiat voluntas tua, etc.*

Followed by the '*Ave Maria, gratia plena.*'

He continued to conduct the service in Latin, and while there was no consecration of the host, the entire crew was fully absorbed in the service. He sprinkled the holy water on all present, making sure it reached everyone. He stopped to pray with each of the sick and dying, blessing them with the holy water and letting them touch or kiss the relic of Saint Francis. He and James led them all in two or three familiar church hymns.

After the service, it was clear to the captain that everyone on the ship, not only the sick and dying but also the healthy crew members, were more at peace with themselves, and there was no more talk of despair among the men.

Francis of Assisi was canonized by Pope Gregory. He is the patron saint of Italy. He received the stigmata in 1224. The stigmata are the appearance of bodily wounds and scars in locations similar to the crucifixion wounds as in the hands, wrists, and feet of Jesus Christ. He was the son of a wealthy merchant. He devoted himself to the church and a life of poverty. Instead of fine clothes, he tonsured his head and wore a coarse woolen tunic tied in the middle with a knotted rope, usually worn by peasants.

He attracted many followers and founded the Franciscan order of monks and nuns with papal approval. His rules were few and simple. First, "follow the teachings of Our Lord Jesus Christ and walk in his footsteps." Second, "to observe the Holy Gospel of Our Lord Jesus Christ, living in obedience without anything of your own and in chastity." He had a great love for birds, animals, and the environment. After his death, his relic was credited with many cures for the sick and disabled.

They were running out of holy water, and the parson was not around to bless any more water. James wondered how his brother was going to get over this problem. Tony simply took a large pail of water from the sea. Then, he produced a little bottle of holy water that Francesco had given each of them to keep them safe on their journey when they set out for Venice. Tony then added a drop of holy water to the large pail of seawater and stirred it well.

Then he explained to James that as he could not take even one drop of the seawater that did not contain at least one molecule of genuine holy water, it was safe to say that every time he sprinkled water from the large pail, everyone and everything it touched was truly blessed. Now, if only he could turn water into wine and multiply loaves and fishes, it would solve a lot of their problems.

Chapter Ten
Man Overboard

The fleet was battered from all sides by the stormy weather and could not maintain its course around the Shetland Islands as planned. By mid-August, the fleet was too far south, sailing between the islands of Orkney to the north and Fair Island to the south. It was stretched out in a long line, with the more sea-worthy ships keeping up the pace and the rest with varying degrees of damage bringing up the rear.

Some had their sails in tatters, others had broken masts, while many had sustained damage to their hull and were lying low in the water and listing badly. As the front runners headed south towards Spain, the Gulf Stream and stormy weather with the strong prevailing winds knocked the entire fleet off course by at least 30 km a day.

By early September, the fleet that had managed to stay together and maintain contact was now scattered, with many ships drifting dangerously close to the coast of Ireland and Scotland. After the storm, the chief commander, Sidonia, reported that 17 ships were unaccounted for. They had simply disappeared.

The Four ships bringing up the rear had fallen further behind. They were severely damaged and letting in more water than they could handle. These ships were the 'Trinidad Valencera,' the 'Barca de Amburgo,' the 'El Gran

Grifon' and the 'Castello Negro'. All four had been separated and had lost all contact with the main body of the fleet. The last report from the 'Barca de Amburgo,' which was right behind the 'Trinidad Valencera,' was that she was taking on water fast and would soon have to be put ashore for repair. The 'Barca de Amburgo,' a transport hulk, was carrying 30 crew members and 233 soldiers.

The 'El Gran Grifon' followed close behind with 43 crew members and 243 soldiers. There was no sign of the 'Castello Negro' a transport hulk. There had been no contact with her for a few days, and it was assumed she was put in somewhere for badly needed repairs and fresh supplies.

The 'Trinidad Valencera,' with 75 crew members and 281 soldiers, had seen more than her fair share of the fighting. The ship was so damaged that it leaked water at every seam. The rigging was reduced to shreds; the main sail had been blown overboard. The decks above and below were littered with debris. The crew were working feverishly, trying to keep the ship afloat. Nobody counted the number of sailors that were swept overboard by the mountainous waves.

James and Tony were thirty to forty feet above deck, working feverously to repair one of the few remaining sails amid lashing rain and the relentless hurricane-force winds. They fearlessly climbed the shroud lines up to the yards as the ship swayed in the gale, walking along the wet and slippery foot-ropes in their bare feet, furling and reefing the sails or what was left of them.

Suddenly and without warning, the foot-rope James and Tony were standing on snapped. James reached out and grabbed the yard he was working on, but Tony lost his balance and fell badly, hitting his head on the way down. He did not call out; there was no flapping about of arms or kicking of legs, no shouts for help. He fell straight into the frigid water of the North Atlantic with a splash. He was lucky he didn't hit the deck below or break his neck on the way down.

James could hear his mother's last words ringing in his ears: "James, look after your brother." Tony was a much stronger swimmer than he was, but he wasn't sure if Tony was even conscious. In any case, he wasn't waiting around to find out. In these waters, you could freeze to death in minutes. He quickly made his way to the end of the yard and dived head-first into the ice-cold water of the North Atlantic Ocean, yelling loud and clear on his way down, hoping someone would hear him and throw him a lifeline.

He aimed to hit the water as close as possible to where Tony went in. He went deep into the darkness, waving and flapping his arms, feeling for anything. He could see nothing in the pitch blackness. He just kept groping around in the freezing water. After a few minutes, he had to come up for air. The ship was moving away fast, being carried by the wind and the current, in what direction nobody was really sure.

Just before James went back down to search for Tony, he caught a glimpse of a small boat being pushed off the main deck into the water, but he had no time for that right now.

He dived repeatedly, going deeper each time, when suddenly he felt something. He was so relieved when he grabbed what was definitely a body and dragged it to the surface as he gasped for air.

On reaching the surface, he realized the body was too thin, much smaller than himself, and not at all as robust as his brother's. This was not Tony but some poor soul who was washed overboard or had died and was buried at sea.

He did not recall any recent burials and then realized that over a hundred Spanish ships had already passed this way ahead of the 'Trinidad Valencera' and all with the same terrible story to tell. He was now drowning in the debts of his existential despair.

He was not going to give up the fight to save his brother. He had wasted too much precious time as it was. He blessed himself with the sign of the cross and prayed to God that 'Tony was still alive.'

He dived once, twice, and repeatedly, each time going deeper. His lungs were hurting, and he was on his way up for air when he felt another body in the cold, icy black water. He grabbed the body and rushed to check if it was Tony.

Then he remembered the cross and chain. He quickly checked, and it was like a sign sent from God himself—a cross with the relic of St Francis of Assisi around his neck. Yes! There it was. He grabbed Tony and dragged him to the surface.

James was well experienced in rescue missions on the mountain, but this was the freezing sea. First, he needed to get Tony to breathe and clear his lungs of any seawater. James clamped his mouth over Tony's and tried to force him to breathe. There was no response. He turned him around and clasped his arms around his brother's rib cage in a strong bear hug.

He tried it repeatedly, a little harder each time, until eventually, Tony spluttered out water and puked into the sea. He began to splash about like a fish out of water. James calmed him down and hugged him tightly, and they both took a minute or two to regain their composure. They started to swim in the boat's direction or where they thought the boat might be.

They were both exhausted and just about ready to give up at any moment, but they kept swimming, slowly but surely, until they reached the boat, bobbing up and down among the waves. As they drew close to the boat, they got a sudden rush of adrenaline, a second wind, and a will to live.

When they reached the boat, James helped Tony in first, and then before he could get in himself, a big wave came out of nowhere and sent him tumbling head over heels away from the boat. When he came to, he was about twenty yards away.

The boat seemed to be moving away with every wave, and he wondered if he would ever see his brother again. He took a deep breath and started swimming again despite his exhaustion and the hopelessness he was feeling.

It seemed the current was pushing them further apart, but he kept trying until he could no longer feel his limbs with the cold. It was then he lost consciousness until he heard his brother shouting his name and dragging him into the boat. The first thing Tony said when he got him in the boat was, "You weren't thinking of leaving me out here all alone, were you now?"

The boat was fitted with a floatation device that kept it upright in the stormy sea. It also had a canvas sheet for protection from the weather, a small survival kit with a candle to signal other boats, hard-tack biscuits to eat and water to drink, a pail, and a small sail and paddle.

All they could do right now was hold each other tight and try to keep from freezing. They stripped off the freezing wet clothes, wrung them out, and tried to dry themselves off. They held each other close, very close, lit the candle for a while, and rubbed each other's limbs to get their blood circulating.

They sheltered under the canvas sheet, ate biscuits, and prayed to God and St Francis of Assisi. They took turns to sleep and rest a little as their boat bobbed up and down on the rolling sea. Despite their plight, they were both thankful to be alive, if only for a few more hours. They hoped that sooner or later, they would be washed up on a shore somewhere. They figured they might be close to the Scottish coast.

That is what they heard the captain say before they fell overboard. They were clever enough to know they were nowhere near to where they should be. The 'Trinidad Valencera' was way, off course. The next day, the storm eased up a little.

They had slept through the night under the canvas. They were both shivering and felt like they were coming down with a fever. They did what they could to keep each other warm, sharing their body heat and rubbing each other hard to keep the blood flowing.

They knew they were getting weaker and weaker, and it was only a matter of time before they would pass out. The only thing they could do now was to pray as they held on tight to the cross that held the relic of St Francis of Assisi. As they grew weaker, they were afraid to fall asleep for fear they might never wake up.

James felt his senses were failing as he looked out over the rim of the small boat bobbing up and down in the water. He thought his eyesight was playing tricks on him when he saw something on the horizon. What started as a blur eventually came into focus. It was definitely a ship. James thought to himself, "They have come back for us."

He quickly mustered what little strength he had left, tied a shirt to the paddle, and waved it in the air as high as he could. As the ship got closer, he could hear the sound of a bell ring. He could also tell it was not the 'Trinidad Valencera' which he knew well. It was a much smaller ship that didn't carry as much sail as the 'Trinidad Valencera.'

Then, they thought it might be one of the English ships still following them. Their hearts sank a little, but as the saying goes, 'any port in a storm,' they were still glad that rescue was on its way. As the ship drew closer, they could see it was not an English ship but a Spanish ship.

It was flying the Spanish Flag with the Imperial Crest of Spain. As the ship came into view, they could see a boat being lowered. Their excitement faded somewhat as the ship drew closer, and they could see it was listing badly on one side. It had obviously taken on more water than it could handle. If they did not put ashore for repairs soon, they would more likely than not have to abandon ship. The bigger question was, "Was she able to make it that far?"

The Ship was the 'Barca de Amburgo'. She had been trailing the 'Trinidad Valencera' for some time and was falling further and further behind. James and Tony were taken on board and checked over by the medics.

It wasn't long before a shot rang out to signal that the 'Barca de Amburgo' could no longer stay afloat and needed urgent assistance. The 'Trinidad Valencera' and the 'El Gran Grifon' were close enough to assist her. Between them, they were able to rescue all on board, including James and Tony.

The 'Trinidad Valencera' and the 'El Gran Grifon' managed to accommodate all survivors from the floundering 'Barca de Amburgo,' which eventually sank somewhere southwest of Fair Island off the coast of Scotland. The storm continued to intensify and was now battering the 'Trinidad Valencera.'

After a few days had passed, they feared the worst for the 'Castillo Negro' and the 'El Gran Grifon.' They had lost contact with both ships. The 'Trinidad Valencera' could not launch a search and rescue mission in her present condition. They were well and truly on their own now. Everyone on board was excited to see James and Tony return safely to the ship except, of course, the 'de Marco' brothers.

They had been staring at James as if in disbelief at what they were seeing and looked away without any expression of relief or gladness on seeing they survived the accident, or was it an accident? James intended to find out for himself. They spent a day or what seemed like a day in recovery, got some food and dry clothes, and were back helping on the rigging. Every able-bodied man was needed. It was all hands on deck if they were to bring this ship home safely.

James wanted to inspect the foot rope they were standing on when Tony fell into the water. He found that all the foot ropes on that yard had been replaced. However, the captain had kept the old foot rope for further inspection. On close examination, one could clearly see the foot rope had been cut right through with a sharp blade, except for a few strands to hold it together.

The captain and James agreed that this was not the time for accusations without proof, but they knew full well who was to blame. The more immediate concern now was that many of the crew and soldiers were seriously sick with fever and food poisoning. They were lying all over the deck, and many among them were dying. The drinking water was contaminated and had a green fungus floating on top; the meat was starting to spoil, and the biscuits were reduced to dust by the weevil. There was no water to spare for the animals on board.

They became restless and posed a real danger to the crew and had to be jettisoned overboard. This was something they did not like doing, but it had to be done. They hoped the animals would be able to swim or be washed ashore by the current. James and Tony spent what time they could tending and caring for the sick and checking if they were comfortable and warm or needed help dressing their wounds.

Tony was trying to comfort a dying sailor who worked on the rigging with Carlos and Luigi. This sailor struggled to speak and was trying to tell him who was responsible for cutting the footrope. Tony thought he was trying to say Carlos, but before he could confirm what happened, he passed away.

Many of the sick had come down with disease and were burning up with fever. They would soak pieces of material in seawater and sponge their brow to cool them down. Water for drinking had to be boiled and then only taken one sip at a time. Many crew members insisted on eating the rotten food to fill their stomachs, if only to bring it back up again.

The 'El Gran Grifton' was a 650-ton transport hulk out of Rostock in Germany. She was also requisitioned by Philip II of Spain to join the fleet to invade England. She was the flagship of the Orca Squadron. She was under the command of Don Juan Gomez de Medina. She had a crew of 43 and carried 243 Spanish soldiers. As a supply transport hulk, she was not expected to participate in the actual fighting; nevertheless, she was fitted with 38 cannons. Unfortunately, at the Battle of Gravelines, she lost her protected position in the Spanish line of defense and sustained several hits.

Seventy men were killed or injured before help came to her rescue. The 'El Gran Grifon' was among the last Spanish ships bringing up the rear and managed to keep pace with the fleet until they rounded the Shetland Islands to head out into the West Atlantic and sail south to Spain.

Though she was overcrowded and in critical need of repair and short on water and food supplies, she answered a distress call from the 'Barca de Amburgo' and helped rescue the crew with the help of the 'Trinidad Valencera.' The abandoned 'Barca de Amburgo' sank shortly thereafter.

In early September, the 'El Gran Grifon' was caught up in stormy weather from the south-west and had no choice, in her weakened condition, but to run before the gale force winds, which blew her north for some time until the wind changed and blew them south again off the west coast of Ireland.

By late September, another storm from the southwest forced them back up past the Hebrides and around Cape Wrath towards the Orkneys. The storm was blowing them back along the route the fleet had taken a month previous. They found themselves headed straight for Fair Island as it appeared right in front of them. The ship barely made it ashore in the rocky cove of Storms Hellier, surrounded by cliffs.

It was not the most suitable place to come ashore, but the captain had very little control over the ship at this stage. The entire crew escaped by climbing up the masts to the cliffs above. The ship stayed afloat long enough to retrieve most of the supplies and equipment that survived the voyage.

The local community shared what little they had with the survivors, which was not nearly enough. The locals were well rewarded for their trouble in gold coins.

Over fifty men, including the captain, did not survive the harsh conditions of the voyage and died from their injuries and disease. They were buried on the Island. Eventually, the rest of the crew eventually made it to the mainland of Scotland and eventually returned to Spain.

Chapter Eleven
Abandon Ship

By mid-September of that year, the 'Trinidad Valencera' was just off the coast of the Inishowen Peninsula on the northern coast of Ireland. She had been battered severely by the weather and had taken on a lot of water. She was listing badly on the starboard side. The captain had no choice but to put ashore and seek help from the local people, whom he hoped would be able to help repair his ship and provide some fresh provisions and water for their voyage back home to Spain.

'The Trinidad Valencera' limped into Kinnagoe Bay on the Inishowen Peninsula and was driven onto the strand at the village of 'Glenagivney' by the storm force winds. Before the crew could disembark, she slipped anchor and was washed back onto the rocks. The captain 'Don Alonso de Luzon' gave the order to 'abandon ship' for fear it would break up on the rocks and sink. Panic set in among the men, and those who could swim jumped overboard.

The captain called for order. There were over 500 men on board, and very few of them were capable of swimming ashore. The captain decided on the order to evacuate. There was only one boat that survived the voyage, and it was less than seaworthy. The first off, the ship, was groups of armed soldiers with their guns at the ready, and it was their job to secure the perimeter.

They were now in unknown territory and did not know what dangers lay ahead. With only one boat, the evacuation was difficult and time-consuming. Starting with the soldiers and officers whose job was to organize the survivors as they came ashore.

The evacuation was slow and orderly until, suddenly, the water began to pour into the ship, causing panic among the men. Some of the sailors were washed overboard, while others jumped into the churning sea and tried to make it to the safety of the shore.

It did not take long before a large boat pulled up alongside the ship. It looked like a welcoming committee of the native Irish chiefs. They had come to make a salvage deal with the captain. A local chieftain of the O'Doherty clan struck a deal to take the men and equipment ashore for payment of 200 gold ducats.

The ship got stuck fast on the rocks, allowing the evacuation to continue. There was no telling when the ship would slip off the rocks and sink. The soldiers were followed by the sick and dying, together with the medics and the caretakers. Shelters were set up along the coastline with canvas sails taken from the ship.

They took whatever they could from the ship. Two days later, she slipped further and was now completely submerged. Much of the ammunition and explosive material was left behind, as was the heavy equipment, including all of the cannons and the three large 40-pound siege cannons specially designed by the famous Belgian Gunsmith "Remigy de Halut" were also left.

The captain knew they would have to move fast to have any chance of making it home to Spain, which meant they had to travel light. The crew and officers were the last to leave the ship. There was a lot of confusion on the shore as the officers struggled to organize the crew and soldiers with all their equipment and supplies.

The sick and wounded were set up in tents, and the very seriously ill and dying were set up in the local church. The soldiers that were still able assembled on the beach as fighting units with their weapons at the ready. When the beach was secure, they fell out in smaller groups and set up separate camps along the coast.

The local community gathered around to help. Food kitchens were set up, and supplies of clean water and fresh food were provided. People were gathering, and the crowds were getting thicker by the minute. The news had traveled fast as if they were expected. It was clear that they were not surprised to see them. The only explanation was they had seen all this before.

Then came the realization that some of the other ships ahead of them had already been forced ashore by the terrible weather that continued to pound the west coast. The 'Trinidad Valencera' was just one of many. The captain was heartened by the news and hoped to meet up with other units that might strengthen their ranks on their journey back home to Spain.

It was not long after that the 'Trinidad Valencera' broke up and sank entirely in the deep water offshore. The local inhabitants provided fresh water and food. James was surprised at the concern many locals displayed as they passed among the sick and dying, offering what little care and comfort they could. None of the locals were able to speak Spanish or Italian. In most cases, they only had a few words of English.

They spoke a rare language with a dialect of their own that they called Gaelic. Many survivors were well beyond help, but the locals tried to make them as comfortable as possible. They helped dress their wounds and provided them with food and water. Tony did what he could to give them spiritual comfort. He continued to wear the monk's habit with the gold cross at the captain's request, as it had a soothing effect on the seriously ill.

As Tony was doing his rounds among the sick, he was relieved to meet up with another Franciscan monk moving through the crowd. It was the local priest by the name of Fr Pius. They both managed to communicate through Latin.

Tony was delighted to be able to talk to a local person in any language and confided how he came to be dressed up as a monk, how the previous pastor had died from his head injury, and how he took his place even though he wasn't ordained.

He told how he had the experience of being brought up in a monastery and how he had a calming effect on the men who were sick. He showed Fr Pius the cross with the relic of St Francis and the rosary beads with the precious stones. Fr Pius put his hand in his pocket, took out a wooden rosary, gave it to Tony, and told him it was dangerous to be seen with anything of value, especially the rosary made of precious stones. People have lost their lives for less.

The wooden rosary had no monetary value, but it was every bit as good in the eyes of the Virgin Mary. He said take it and use it, and I hope it will keep you safe. After they spoke for a while, Fr Pius grabbed Tony by the arm and whispered in Latin, "Listen carefully to what I am about to tell you." He told him they were all in terrible danger and things were not as they seemed.

Ships had already broken up along the coast; he was sorry to say the survivors were not well treated by the local people or those loyal to the English. Most, if not all, were robbed of their meager possessions and murdered in cold blood.

The English authorities in Ireland offered a reward for the capture and execution of all Spanish survivors and severe penalties for anyone caught harboring or helping them in any way. Pius told Tony that he and his companions should be on their guard and be prepared and ready, as there was danger all around.

There were spies everywhere. Trust no one, and do not mistake acts of kindness as genuine acts of friendship. He also told Tony that should he make it through all of this and need help, he should return to the church after midnight. The side door would be left open. It was unwise for them to speak for long as they were being watched, and he needed to be on his way.

Still speaking in Latin, Fr Pius blessed him and bade him farewell with God's blessing. Tony tried to keep his calm and refrained from over reacting to what he just heard. He continued what he was doing for the next five to ten minutes. As he looked around at the crowds of people getting larger by the hour, he looked closely at their faces. He started to see compassion and empathy in some.

Still, in others, he started to see a different side of humanity that comes from greed and treachery with the excitement and anticipation of a scavenger before it finally takes down its victim. He felt that they were watching his every move, waiting for him to panic and try to escape before they made their move to cut him off and go in for the kill.

He then made his way slowly to where James was helping the medics. Tony conveyed news of the warning to James as discreetly as possible. He warned that they were being watched constantly; there were spies everywhere that meant them harm.

They knew that going straight to the captain could raise suspicions that could trigger a riot among the crowd, putting the whole crew in imminent danger. They had to find a way to tell the captain without raising any alarms.

They needed a good excuse to meet with the captain in private. With that, James noticed the captain was moving among the sick men, giving words of encouragement and comfort. James went to one of the sick men he could trust, one the captain was sure to visit because of his serious condition. His job was to tell the captain that James and Tony had information of the utmost importance to report and that secrecy was vital as they were under constant scrutiny.

They needed to talk to him in the privacy of his tent and that he, the captain, was not to show any surprise or change of expression that might raise suspicion. There were spies everywhere, and it was a matter of life and death that they should meet as soon as possible. James motioned to the captain, indicating that this man was very sick and needed a consoling word.

The captain nodded his consent and slowly made his way in that direction. When the captain arrived at his side, James took the captain's assistant aside, leaving the captain alone with the sick man, who wasted no time relaying the message to the captain as he was instructed.

The captain praised the ill man on a job well done and continued his rounds, passing a fleeting glance at James. An indication that the message was received loud and clear. The captain agreed to see both James and Tony in his tent within the hour. James replied with a nod. James had not yet heard the whole story Tony had to relate, but he knew his brother well enough and trusted him without question.

If what he had to say was so important, it didn't bear telling twice. He would wait for the captain to be present. The hour felt more like a day, and when they finally made their way to the captain's tent, they took their time and stopped here and there along the way to comfort the sick, showing no urgency, no cause for alarm.

On entering the tent, they were welcomed by the captain and his first officer, who inquired what all the secrecy was about. The captain was very calm and open-minded to what he was about to hear. He trusted the two brothers and felt they wouldn't ask for this meeting unless it was really important. They all listened to what Tony had to say with quiet disbelief.

The captain put his head in both hands and momentarily dropped his elbows to the table before he spoke. Sidonia had warned them that something like this could happen. While they could no longer rely on the crews from other ships to help them, he had to keep his options open. He had to keep his soldiers together and ready to engage the enemy at a moment's notice.

There was always the chance that some crews could still make it ashore further along the coast. They might need his help as much as he needed theirs. They would travel south along the west coast as far as possible. He was also aware that the local Irish did not like the English in some areas and might be sympathetic to the Spanish in the hope of one day forcing the English from their homeland. However, they would have to rely on their own resources for now. They were truly on their own.

The captain ordered that every fighting man be put on alert and be prepared and ready for battle at a minute's notice. They would use whatever little time they had to recover from the ordeals of the voyage that brought them to this God-forsaken part of the world. Officers were to advise the troops not to trust or confide in any of the locals as it was vital to their survival that silence be maintained at all times.

He was aware that his soldiers were in no condition to fight, but he wanted to present a well-trained, formidable force of fighting men. Appearance was everything. Now, at least, they knew what to expect and what they were up against. If it was gold they were looking for, he was going to make it difficult for them.

He would distribute whatever gold there was among the soldiers and crew as payment for their services. Some officers suggested the gold should be kept to bargain with the English, but the captain responded that the people they are now dealing with don't bargain; they take.

His orders were to be carried out discreetly and quietly and to warn the men to be careful and keep their money out of sight of prying eyes and warn them of the danger of loose talk even among themselves.

Also, if the situation becomes untenable, he gave his blessing to any man trying to make it back home. They would not be charged with desertion. He was aware that he was not in a position to guarantee any man's safety.

James and Tony went about their business tending to the injured and the dying. Food was being supplied by the locals, for which they were well paid. Tony continued to play his role as a spiritual advisor and spent a lot of time giving comfort to those who needed it. Disease was spreading rapidly, and the brothers were well aware of the signs, having watched both their parents die in this very same way all those years ago. They were not likely to forget the hopelessness they experienced, and they felt a special bond with those who wouldn't make it home to Spain and their families.

Wounds were starting to fester, but all they could do to help was to keep them clean. They had clean hot water now, good food, and clean bandages, which was a big help, but for some, the help had come too late. The two brothers knew that the worst was yet to come, but for now, they would stay calm and be prepared to act at a moment's notice.

Chapter Twelve
Elagh Castle

The English Crown was aware that many of the native Irish were sympathetic to the Spanish and would be happy to help them get back home to Spain. They were also afraid the Spanish would join the Irish rebels against the forces of the Crown in Ireland.

The English Lord Deputy in Ireland was misinformed by London that the entire Spanish fleet was planning to launch an all-out attack on England from the west coast of Ireland. It ordered that all Spanish soldiers were to be shot on sight and anyone caught harboring or helping them to be charged as traitors to the Crown. They were also advised that armed reinforcements were on their way from London and were expected to be landing soon to take command of the situation and deal with any traitors.

Captain Don Alonzo de Luzon of the 'Trinidad Valencera' planned to march south in the hope that he might meet up with other Spanish survivors who would help bolster his ranks. The O'Doherty chieftains promised that they would be met at 'Burt Castle' by sympathetic native Irish who would help them get back home to Spain. 'Burt Castle,' an O'Doherty stronghold, was about a five-day march south.

Captain Luzon was anxious to get his men on the move and saw no point in waiting around in Inishowen. He gave the order to prepare to pull out.

Equipment and supplies were loaded up for the journey. Carts pulled by mules were organized to carry the sick. The officers and soldiers took up a marching formation with their guns at the ready. They wore their helmet and breastplates with the Spanish insignia on their surcoat. They had their bayonets attached and had every appearance of a formidable fighting force ready and eager to fight and not a shipwrecked army on their last legs.

They had no cannon or large artillery and were unsure if they had enough dry powder for their muskets. They were followed by the medics and the sick at the rear of the column. The captain, his second in command, and the O'Doherty chieftain led on horseback. They stretched out along the narrow road in a slow parade. James and Tony stayed at the rear of the column with the sick where they were most useful.

Very few, if any, were able to read or write. James and Tony were supplied with writing material by the captain and spent their time helping the sick and dying by writing letters to the wives and sweethearts back home. They wondered if the warning from Fr Pius was true and if any of these letters would ever make it back to Spain. Some of the very sick left the letters with Tony for safekeeping. Tony made sure he had names and addresses for each and every one.

After a seven-day march, they arrived at 'Burt Castle,' but they were not met by sympathizers but by a regiment of militia soldiers loyal to the England Crown under the command of Richard and Henry Hovenden, who were foster brothers of the Irish chieftain 'Hugh O'Neill,' Earl of Tyrone who was a staunch ally of the English Crown.

A battle ensued, and the Spanish, who were ill-prepared for battle and totally outgunned, were forced to surrender and lay down their arms with the promise of safe passage to Dublin. However, the captors were only interested in the officers who could be ransomed off for money or used in a prisoner exchange with Spain.

Forty-five noblemen and Officers were separated from the rest of the men and force marched to the capital to surrender to the lord Deputy, where they would be shipped to London to be held for ransom.

However, on the way, they were beaten and robbed of their valuables. Many did not make it to the capital alive. The rest of the soldiers and crew were taken to Elagh Castle, the current residence and stronghold of the O'Doherty Clan. They arrived there at nightfall and were herded into a courtyard surrounded by high walls. The entrance was heavily guarded.

The prisoners were tired, hungry, and weary after their journey. Many were still suffering from their injuries. Others were sick with disease and fever. They were still lying on the carts and wagons used to transport them on the journey. The animals that pulled the carts had been taken away and put out in a field close by. The night was bitterly cold, and the courtyard did not offer much shelter from the elements.

James and Tony were still looking after the sick and wounded when James noticed a length of rope on one of the carts. This gave him cause to think about mountain climbing back home in the Alps. It wasn't long before a plan to climb the wall started to take shape. James talked it over with Tony, and both agreed it was worth trying. It was not long before the guards started taking prisoners out one at a time to be interrogated and searched. The prisoners were stripped and searched before being returned to the courtyard.

They told the others on their return that their valuables and gold coins were confiscated. However, that soon stopped, and those taken out were no longer returned after being searched. The guards quickly realized the prisoners were leaving their money and valuables behind with comrades for safekeeping. It was assumed that those not returned were being murdered.

They had no officers to lead them, but a few soldiers stepped forward as leaders of the group. They decided that rushing the guards was their only chance of escape. They all agreed they would do so at the first opportunity. However, there were many among them who knew they were too weak and too sick to run for their lives in a country where they were not familiar with the terrain and could not speak the language. They would take their chances with their captors rather than slow down the others. They were still willing to rebel and do whatever it took to help their comrades escape.

Some of the more seriously ill wanted Tony to hear their last confession, and a few also wanted to donate their possessions to the church. Tony did what he could do to help them through their final hours, knowing that they might not make it home. James, having considered the plan of a mass escape, was not convinced it would work, having considered the language difficulty and the lack of directions.

They decided to go it alone and climb the wall. Their plan, though dangerous and risky, was to climb over the high wall in the dark of night. They could hide on top and wait for the opportunity to escape when the coast was clear. They would use their contact with Father Pius to escape by ship and make their way back home to Venice. They did not let any of the others know exactly what they were planning to do other than to say they were going to escape.

The fact that they would be hiding up there on the rampart for any length of time was not something they wanted everyone to know. They needed to do it quietly, but they also wanted to say goodbye and wish their comrades well.

They had a bad feeling that they might not see their friends again if what Fr. Pius told them was true. They could not tell the others what they knew for fear it would cause a panic, and who knows if it was true or just hearsay. In any case, they were going to stick with their own plan of escape.

Some of the prisoners insisted James and Tony take the gold coins they had received from the captain rather than have them stolen by the militia. All they asked was that they put the gold to good use if they managed to escape. As the night went by, the prisoners started settling down, and a quietness came over the crowd as they started to fall asleep.

Having said their goodbyes, the two brothers started up the wall, staying in the shadows. They traveled light and stayed close to the corner, which was safer and easier than the open face. They took their time and carefully executed each move. Progress was slow at first, but as the night went on, they gradually climbed higher and higher. Their fingers were cut to the bone on the rough stone wall. They continued up the wall until they disappeared into the shadows above.

The brothers were experienced climbers and were well aware of the risks in 'free solo climbing' the wall of a castle. Other than a length of rope taken from the cart, they had no proper climbing equipment, nor did they have metal spikes to hammer into the cracks for a secure hold that would support their weight. They had no harnesses or spiked footwear; they relied solely on their own individual strength and skill. They knew how important it was to remain focused.

Any slip without a safety harness could be fatal. This escape was something they felt they could do, as the alternative did not bear thinking about. The wall was well eroded from years of neglect and disrepair, leaving plenty of footholds, making it relatively easy to climb. The ascent was going well until they got within fifteen feet of the top of the wall. To continue their climb, they needed proper climbing gear.

They could not get a grip on the wall, not even a finger hold, between the close-knit limestone rocks without some sort of a pick or spike. They needed to get beyond the next few feet before proceeding to the top. They were so close and yet so far away.

There was one small crack, but they needed something hard to chip away at the mortar. Their fingers were sore from scraping with the gold coins, but that did not have much effect in opening up this crack. Despair started to set in when James realized the solution was staring at him in the face. He did not like the idea of desecrating the holy cross, especially one bearing the relic of Saint Francis, but this was a matter of life and death.

Tony handed over the cross, and James hacked away at a crack until he could get a good deep finger grip hold big enough to get them up to the next level. The cross suffered minor damage, which was regrettable but unavoidable under the circumstances. Tony called it divine intervention in how the cross kept getting them out of trouble; however, James took a more rational view of it.

They made it up to the rampart, where they could rest for a while, well out of sight of the others, where they could see over the wall without any danger of being spotted by the militia. They would be safe here for the night. The exterior side of the wall was so weather-beaten by the northwest winds that the gaps between the stones were bigger and deeper.

James could see that birds were even nesting in the crevices. He reckoned that the wider spaces between the stones would make the descent much easier and faster. Right now, they were staying out of sight.

After some time, two soldiers stepped out onto the rampart. They appeared to have been drinking as they staggered to the edge and started to urinate on the prisoners down below. The brothers moved back into the shadows, and in a quiet corner of the rampart, they slowly lowered themselves down just over the exterior of the wall using the rope.

They hoped the rope was not noticed by the soldiers as they walked about on the rampart before they left. However, many more soldiers were guarding the prisoners down below. It would soon be light, so they decided to stay out of sight and spend the day on the wall till it was dark enough to escape with fewer soldiers.

They heard some commotion on the other side of the wall. They had a bird's eye view and could see everything with the campfire's light. A few soldiers were beating and yelling at one of the prisoners. They were yelling at him in English, but he obviously could not understand what they were saying.

James and Tony couldn't understand neither, but they were clearly looking for anything valuable. Fr Pius had told them that the other ships that ran aground suffered the same abuse by the militia in search of gold. Everyone had heard of the ships filled with gold and treasure from the

Americas, and they were told of gold coins being recovered from the survivors of other Spanish shipwrecks along the coast.

They stripped him naked and searched his clothes until they found what they were looking for. The gold coins were hidden in the leather folds of his boots. They beat him up pretty severely, and then they took him to an area off to the side, away from the castle. The two militia returned alone; it was obvious they had murdered him quietly as they did not want to waste a bullet.

They then took out another prisoner, and the same thing happened. This was repeated well into the night with many more prisoners before daybreak. That was when one of their commanders arrived with more soldiers to relieve them.

Later in the morning, all the prisoners were marched out into a field beside the castle, and that is when it all happened. Some of the men started fighting among themselves, and when the guards tried to stop them, the prisoners, who outnumbered the guards at least twenty to one, started pushing and shoving until the militia could no longer control them.

The prisoners stormed the guards, who were easily overrun. Some of the guards were relieved of their firearms. A large number of the prisoners escaped and ran off in all directions. Shots rang out, and several prisoners were shot dead. It took some time before reinforcements with sniffer dogs arrived on the scene to help the guards.

Without arms and directions, it did not take long before most of the prisoners were rounded up and brought back to the castle. The armed guard had been doubled, and the dogs were going crazy, viciously snapping at the heels of the prisoners. They were all stripped, and their clothing was searched, relieving them of anything of value, including their gold coins.

They were then taken aside in groups and massacred in broad daylight. Some were shot with muskets, and others had their throats slit with the blade. There was no limit to the debts of depravity the militia stooped to. James and Tony found it difficult to watch their fellow human beings treated this way, especially those they had gotten to know when attending to the sick and wounded or working alongside on the rigging.

Fr Pius was right; he had tried to warn them. He was the one and only person they knew they could trust. He might be their best hope of escaping and returning to Spain or Italy. They were definitely going back to the church to make contact with him, but first, they had to get back to the coast.

James threw his arms around his brother and hugged him hard, reassuring him again that they were going to make it back alive. Someone had to live to tell the world what had happened here today. The brothers made themselves comfortable on the wall and settled down until it was dark enough to make a move. Luckily for them, there were no guards on the rampart keeping watch. They did not see the need.

It would be a long wait until the sun went down, and they would be safe to steal away in the silence of the night now that every available militia soldier was out searching for escaped prisoners. They were both suffering from shock and sick to their stomachs at what they had seen that day. They needed some quiet time alone to get their heads around the horrors they witnessed.

They needed to put all that behind them and focus on the task ahead. The clothes taken from the prisoners were carefully searched for valuables and discarded at the base of the wall. James suggested they should check them out and see if they could use anything on their journey back to the coast.

Just then, two soldiers arrived down below. They placed their muskets to one side and sat down beside a burning brazier. James recognized them from earlier when they took prisoners out one by one and robbed and murdered them. They were drinking some kind of homemade whisky. They made themselves comfortable and were settling in for the night. They counted their spoils and put the gold coins into small leather bags.

When they had finished counting, they started checking the discarded clothes, obviously looking for more gold that might have been missed by the others. They didn't find any more gold, but anything of value they did find, they laid it out in a neat pile. There were a few flints for lighting fires, some food that was being saved for the journey home that would never happen, some bread and cheese, some pieces of clothing, waterproof oil skin jackets, and a few garments that might be useful.

As the light started to fade, the brothers decided it was dark enough to climb down the wall without being noticed. They wanted to be ready to make their escape when an opportunity presented itself. As they were climbing down, Tony disturbed a bird's nest. A seagull came screeching straight out of its nest and straight into his face. He got such a fright he missed his footing and slipped.

As he dropped, James was able to grab him long enough for him to regain a grip on the wall. They both froze as they looked at the two soldiers who were now staring at the wall, wondering what all the commotion was about. One soldier walked over to the wall in time to see the seagull make its way back to its nest while James and Tony hugged the shadows on the wall well out of sight in the darkness of the night.

"Just another lover's quarrel," he exclaimed, returning to his seat beside the fire. After they were able to get their breath back, James and Tony continued to climb down to the base of the wall as quietly as possible, staying in the shadows as much as they could. They had just about reached the bottom of the wall when two dogs with their handlers appeared on the scene. The dogs started acting up and barking furiously. They immediately raced to the wall and began sniffing about.

The two brothers scampered back up the wall, taking two strides at a time back into the shadows. One of the handlers asked what was exciting the dogs and what they were after. The other suggested it was the scent of the old clothes stacked up against the wall. Maybe they smell all the gold, said one of the guards. The dog handlers replied that there was not much of that left as they had been checking for gold earlier in the day and had done a thorough job.

They were off to bed as they had been out looking for prisoners for hours and needed to rest before going out again. They would lock the dogs up, which should keep them quiet, suggested one of the handlers.

The two brothers waited for a while to settle their nerves before they made their way down to the base of the wall for the second time that night. The two militia soldiers were oblivious to what was happening at the wall. The brothers knew that they would have to take out the two soldiers if they had any chance of getting away without being noticed. They needed something they could use as a weapon, but Tony refused to allow the cross to be desecrated in that way. They would have to rely on their martial arts skill.

They had the element of surprise on their side apart from the fact that the two militia soldiers were drunk on cheap whiskey. When the two brothers moved in unison, the soldiers had no chance to use their muskets and raise the alarm. They were taken out silently with the speed and efficiency of two ninja warriors. They had to move fast; there was no telling when more handlers with dogs might arrive.

They dragged the two bodies away from the light of the fire, stripped them of their uniforms, and laid their bodies face down among the dead prisoners that had been stripped and murdered earlier on. They had to do it in such a way that the two soldiers would not be easily missed or noticed for some time. The one thing they did not want was for the bodies to be found too soon and for the militia to track them down with sniffer dogs before they could get far enough away.

Chapter Thirteen
Burt Castle

Tony was pleased the two soldiers had already sorted out the contents of the prisoner's discarded clothes. It had saved them a lot of valuable time. They organized a neat bundle of useful items for each to carry, as well as some food items and, of course, all of the gold and valuables. Having cleaned up the area as best they could and not wasting any precious time, they headed out into the night.

They took the uniforms and muskets with them, and when they were a safe distance from 'Elagh Castle,' they put on the militia breastplate and helmet and slung the muskets over their shoulder. The local people would not think it strange to see two soldiers out searching for escaped prisoners in the dark of night. They were in unchartered territory and decided that they would go back to Burt Castle first since they knew the way and which was not too far.

From there, they were confident they could find their way back to the coast. However, the early morning light was starting to break in the east. James thought it best to hide and rest during the day and travel at night. It would take another day or two to 'Burt Castle.' They would travel at night when all the roads were clear, and they could make good time. There would be less chance of being met on the road and appearing suspicious in uniforms splattered with blood and not fitting very well.

They felt terrible about how they killed the two soldiers, but after what they witnessed that day, they felt wholly justified in their actions, both in the eyes of God and man. They had the cover of the uniforms, but they would take no chances of being stopped and recognized. It was only a matter of time before the two missing soldiers would be found, and the militia would be looking for two fugitives in uniform.

They knew they would have to get rid of the uniforms soon. The uniforms were not a good fit anyway and were very uncomfortable. Nothing would please Tony more than to get rid of them. The uniforms were dirty and covered with blood stains. The blood stains that only served to remind him of the massacre of his comrades and friends.

Having traveled for hours, the sky was overcast, and the wind was getting stronger. They finally caught sight of 'Burt Castle' in the distance. The air was moist as it had rained earlier. The distinctive musky petrichor scent was heavy in the air as they made their way along the narrow grassy lane, lined with stone walls on either side covered with brambles laden with blackberries.

James and Tony ate their fill of the juicy fruit to appease their hunger as they went on their way. The walls provided a place to hide to avoid talking to over inquisitive strangers they might meet along the road. As they got close to Burt Castle, the weather changed for the worse. There was a heavy downpour, and within minutes, they were soaked through to the skin.

There was no sign of life anywhere in or around the Castle. It seemed to be deserted. Their first instinct was to avoid the place altogether and continue until they found shelter somewhere safer.

On the other hand, it was still dark, and they were soaked right through and needed to get shelter from the rain and dry themselves off before they got pneumonia. As everyone seemed to have vacated Burt Castle in favor of Elagh Castle, where all the action was, the brothers decided to check it out.

The castle was surrounded by a dried-up moat. They watched the castle from a safe distance for some time before venturing closer. They managed to gain entry to the castle through an unlocked side entrance. The Castle was overrun with rats that seemed to have eaten any food the previous occupants had left behind.

The whole building reeked of human feces and urine. The presence of cleaning equipment led one to believe an attempt was being made to prepare the building for a new occupant or the return of the old. Having checked each floor, making sure there was no one else in the building, they went on a scavenger hunt for something to eat.

All they could find was a barrel of apples. Tony checked the outbuildings and arrived back with a handful of eggs. There was plenty of water and a few stoneware jugs of wine. They relaxed and settled down to their first decent meal for some time. They swallowed the eggs raw with the little food they brought with them.

The wine was not quite what they were used to, but nevertheless, they drank a whole jug. They were not sure when or what their next meal would be, but for now, they were both satisfied and content.

There were plenty of outbuildings where they could shelter outside the castle's walls, but they found a room on the third floor where they could keep watch for anybody coming in the distance. The three-story castle was built on a hill. Anybody approaching the castle could be spotted for miles off. It was a good place to shelter and freshen up, get some sleep, eat some food, and build up their strength.

The militia would be busy combing the countryside, searching for runaway prisoners for the next few days. The filthy condition of the castle led the brothers to believe that nobody would bother them any time soon, and besides, what better place to be hiding than in the castle itself?

Nobody would ever suspect to find them there. There was plenty of water to wash off the grime and dirt of the last few days. They changed back into their own dry clothes that fit better. They were happy to discard the breastplate and helmet, which were anything but comfortable to wear. They believed they would be quite safe to hold up in the castle for the night.

There was a wooded area behind the castle that would help hide their escape if they were forced to flee, should they have any surprise visitors. They would take turns standing watch. They were both exhausted after their journey and needed to sleep. James took the first watch, but after a couple of hours, he felt drowsy from drinking too much wine and was having difficulty staying awake.

He must have nodded off for a few hours at least, for when he awoke, he could hear other people moving about in the castle. He could see that the daylight was already coming through the window. He must have been asleep for hours. He could feel the cold sweat on his brow and was numb all over. He had screwed up in the worst possible way; he had let his brother down.

He recalled his promise to his dying mother 'to look after his brother.' He had to pull himself together; this was no time to lose his nerve. He did not know how many others were in the castle.

If he had been awake, he would have seen them coming and would know precisely how many of them there were. So far, he could only hear two or three. He gently woke Tony, who had been sound asleep in a corner of the room. With a finger on his lips, he signaled the danger to Tony, who quickly rose to his feet.

James sneaked over to the door to get a closer look. In the dim light, he could make out one soldier. He could tell they had been drinking from the sound of their voices. He could hear a second soldier close by, relieving himself in the adjacent room. He listened for others but did not hear anyone else, not on this floor anyway.

James's guess was they were drunk, having been up drinking all night like the two soldiers they had to kill back at 'Elagh Castle' and now needing a place to sleep it off. He still could not rely on these two being here alone. He was relieved they were not searching for escaped prisoners here in the castle. As they were right in the next room, they were blocking any chance of escape without being noticed. He had to assume that there were others nearby! He could not risk using the muskets they took from 'Elagh Castle' as that would alert any other soldiers in or outside the castle.

As their escape route was blocked, they had to decide whether to wait it out or make a run for it. Either way, there was the chance that they might be caught and shot trying to escape. Then, the old wooden floor made a creaking noise loud enough to be heard by the soldier in the next room. The soldier took out his pistol and called out, "Whoever was there to come out and show themself, or he would blow their brains out."

James could not understand the language, but there was no mistaking the message. James needed time to think. He did not want to inflame the situation with the soldier letting off a shot. He glanced at Tony and put a finger to his lips not to make a sound. Then he stood up and walked into the light with his hands in the air.

At that moment, he wished he was still wearing the militia uniform. It might have given him a chance to get the drop on the soldier with the pistol pointed right at him. The big burly soldier punched James hard in the ribs while holding a pistol to his head with the other hand, and when James slumped to the floor in pain, the soldier hit him across the head with the butt of his gun. James lay on the floor, holding his stomach in pain.

He felt the rage building up inside him. He had not come this far to be stopped now. The soldier had relaxed his weapon now that he had James lying on the floor, doubled up in pain. At that moment, Tony appeared in a uniform coat, holding a musket at the door. The soldier grabbed his pistol again and aimed it right at Tony, who did not hesitate to discharge his musket first.

The soldier dropped his pistol and fell to the floor beside James. At the sound of the musket, the other soldier came running in and, seeing what had happened, pointed his musket at Tony, who did not have time to reload. James gritted his teeth and took a deep breath, and having mustered all his strength, he grabbed the pistol from the floor beside him and, with careful aim, shot the second soldier and prayed to God that there was no one else in the castle.

With no sign of anybody else, James and Tony both gave a sigh of relief. They checked for vital signs before tossing the two dead bodies out the open window onto the marshy ground in the moat below.

James and Tony knew they needed to get away fast before more soldiers arrived. Staying at the castle was a bad idea. They packed as many apples as they could carry. They left the muskets and the uniforms behind since they were too heavy to carry, and they did not envision getting into a full-scale fight with the militia.

They did, however, take the pistol. It was one of the latest flintlock models with a supply of paper cartridges. The letters C J C were engraved on the stock. The owner must have been an officer, maybe a captain. They had no time to lose; it was a long way to the coast, and they could only travel at night. James felt they could hide out along the coast and live off the land when they got there. With a bit of luck, they may be able to get a ship across to Scotland and maybe work their way home on a ship from there. After all, they were sailors.

It was quite some distance from 'Burt Castle' back to the coast where Fr. Pius had offered to help them. It certainly would take them six or seven days, especially traveling only at night and resting during the day. They would hide wherever they could find a place, sometimes in a wooded area, sometimes in a deserted shed or house, and often in the ruins of old buildings.

One night, they happened upon an empty cottage that had been temporally vacated by the owner. There was still food in the pantry and clothes in the wardrobe. James and Tony borrowed two overcoats to cover up their Italian-style dress and allow them to fit in better with the local community. Nobody would be expecting them to return to the coast. It would be more likely for sailors on the run to be fleeing in the opposite direction.

They were anxious to meet up with Fr Pius and find out what he could do to help them. They pushed themselves to travel a bit further every night and made it to the coast in record time. The sea air was refreshing, and they did not have to worry about prying eyes in the dark of night. There was freedom in the air, and they felt good. They were going to make it work. James remembered a few places along the coast where they might be able to hide while waiting to meet up with Fr. Pius.

When they reached the coast, the sun was rising in the east, but there was still no sign of people moving about on the beach. There were plenty of makeshift shelters, and a few fires were still burning. This gave the two brothers time to find someplace to hide for a few hours, a place to rest and plan their next move. In another hour or two, the beach would be swarming with scavengers.

All of them digging in the sand, looking for anything they could salvage, hoping to find some gold from the Spanish treasure ships they had heard so much about. All sorts of stuff were being washed ashore, including the bodies of dead sailors. Their clothing was being searched by people who were frantically hoping to find pieces of gold or jewelry, and even the articles of clothing that had no monetary value were taken as souvenirs.

It was too risky to go to the church to meet Fr Pius in the daylight as the militia were everywhere and would most likely be watching the church. They feared someone would recognize them from when they first came ashore and turn them in. They continued further west along the coastline until they came to a secluded spot away from the main road with lots of shelter.

There was a boathouse that seemed to be locked up for the winter. It was well boarded up, but some of the wood was old and rotten. They had no trouble breaking in. There was an unusual-looking boat propped up on blocks. It was built with a wooden frame covered with animal hide. It had a shallow bottom and no keel. It was sturdy and strong and incredibly light and easy to handle. They had seen the local people use similar boats when they first came ashore, but this was the first time they saw it up close.

There were also oars, some old fishing nets, and lots of stoneware jars, but most of all, there was protection from the cold northwest wind blowing down from the Arctic. They made themselves as comfortable as possible. Their first chance to rest since they left 'Burt Castle.' Now, they had time to rethink their strategy and plan their next move.

They felt they would be safe in the boathouse for a few days. There was a freshwater stream close by. The shore would provide some crabs and mussels. They might be able to catch fish using the nets they found in the boathouse. James was sure he could snare or trap a few rabbits or maybe a few wild birds.

They felt they would be safe here for a few days. They could even light a fire like so many of the treasure seekers were doing, but they had to be careful and be as discrete as possible. They were better off on their own, away from the over-curious crowds. They counted out the gold coins, and there were over five hundred in all; with additional pieces of personal jewelry taken from the prisoners back at Elagh Castle, there were even a few gold teeth.

It was getting too heavy to carry around. They needed to hide it somewhere safe, along with the crucifix and the rosary! There were too many people moving around to venture out in the open. They would have to wait until all the excitement died down. After a few days, they would try to contact Fr. Pius.

The next day, James watched as the treasure seekers spread out along the shore in the hope of finding bodies washed up on the beach, as what happened with other Spanish wrecks further west.

Looking out to sea, James noticed an island in the distance. He suggested to Tony that they row out to the island under the cover of darkness and check it out. If they liked it, they could stay a day or two. Otherwise, they could be back before morning. There was nothing to lose and everything to gain. Nobody would bother them out there, and they would be free to light a fire without anybody noticing.

They gathered their things and filled the boat with whatever they could use. They took a fishing net and some fishing tackle that they found lying around the boathouse. They also took some empty stoneware jugs and metal boxes that they could use to boil water or store food. They pushed the boat out beyond the breakers and into the calm waters beyond the waves.

The sky was overcast, the evening was quite dark, and a mist came in from the sea. They would not be noticed; if they were, they would easily be mistaken as local fishermen. It took them less than an hour to reach the far side of the island.

Chapter Fourteen
The Island

High cliffs surrounded the island and were home to many different species of sea birds. Tony wondered how they all survived the harsh conditions of the North Atlantic. They had not seen many of these birds up close before in real life, other than in library books. There were Puffins with their orange beaks, black and white terns, gannets, gulls, and guillemots, all competing for the same fish as James and Tony—no need to say who was better at catching fish.

James's first thought was how he could catch the birds and what they would taste like; he already knew how to fish. On the boat ride over, they had cast the net out over the end of the boat and dragged it behind them. Their efforts were rewarded with three good-sized sea bass.

They found a small cove with a sandy beach between the cliffs that was well sheltered from the elements. They dragged the boat ashore, hid it among the rocks, and covered it with seaweed. There was a log cabin on the Island just above the sandy beach that had obviously been left to the mercy of the elements for many a year and had long since been vacated in favor of the mainland.

They had brought some stoneware jugs of fresh water with them from the coast. James noticed that there was a plentiful supply of spring water flowing from the cliffs which they didn't need now, but it was good to keep in mind should they want to pay a return visit to the island at a later date. It was the perfect place to rest up for a day or two. The cabin door was locked, but the lock was anything but secure. The door itself was falling apart. Why anyone would go to the trouble of putting a lock on it was a mystery. It was likely more of a privacy notice 'to keep out' rather than a security measure.

It took no more than a few minutes before they were comfortably inside the confines of the shack. In the dim light that seeped through the many gaps in the timber, James noticed more stoneware jugs neatly packed on shelves in one corner of the cabin, the exact same type as those back on the mainland. He wondered what they were used for. He assumed they were also empty, as were the jars back at the boathouse.

As they were on the far side of the island, they felt safe in lighting a small fire with driftwood they found on the beach and using the flint they salvaged from 'Elagh Castle.' They managed to cook their fish, which tasted absolutely delicious; as the saying goes, "hunger is the best sauce." There were a lot of fishing nets stored in the cabin, which they could use for bedding.

The nets were very comfortable to lie on, and the brothers felt secure and safe as they nestled down for the night. They were glad of the extra clothes they brought with them from 'Elagh Castle' as they bundled up to keep themselves warm. Tomorrow, they would explore the rest of the Island in the daylight.

The following morning, they awoke with the lark. They were well-rested and refreshed. They went for a swim in the North Atlantic Ocean, cooked some fish for breakfast, and for a few brief hours, they forgot all their worries and cares. The first order of business was to do a tour of the Island. It was a nice, fresh morning with a slight breeze blowing in from the sea.

The island was a lot bigger than it appeared from the shore. James was delighted when he came across a few rabbit warrens. There were a few soft black droppings around the burrow entrance, which indicated some rabbit activity during the night. He would put down a few traps, hoping to snare something they could cook over the campfire to eat other than fish.

In the middle of the island, there was a huge chestnut tree that was hollow in the center. It was obvious that the tree was used to shelter campfires from the weather as it was well-scorched and blackened on one side.

The hollow center was nearly big enough for a person to fit inside. There were plenty of other trees on the island, but this tree stood out on its own in the middle of a clearing. It would be easy to find if they ever came back. It was the perfect place to hide the gold. They put all the valuables into a tin box and placed it in the hollow tree. They leaned right in and placed it up on a ledge where it was hard to reach. It would be safe there until they needed to get it again.

They found another shack that was also locked. It was every bit as easy to break into. There were some loose boards that were easy to remove. It was probably used for keeping animals at one time. It would be a good fallback shelter if needed.

On looking closer, James saw something he recognized straight away. He had seen it often enough back at the monastery. It was equipment for brewing and distilling alcohol. The monks were always brewing and winemaking and liked to experiment with new concoctions and recipes of their own.

They liked trying different fruits and grains in the hope of inventing that special beverage. It is generally accepted that the art of distilling was started by Christian monks in the Middle East around the sixth century. There was evidence of distilling in Ireland around the twelfth century. Every household would make their own alcoholic brew using a small pot. Hence the name poteen, meaning a small pot in the native Irish language.

Poteen was regarded as a cure for almost all ailments, especially the flu and the common cold. It was the preferred beverage at any celebration, especially at wakes, marriages, and christenings. They would also make their own beer and an alcoholic drink made from honey they called 'mead.'

In later years, entrepreneurial individuals with exceptional brewing talent would set up their own brewing business to serve the wider community. Each distiller had their own recipe, and they guarded it with their life. They all used the same ingredients, more or less, but they would use their own special mix, which was a well-kept secret. Originally the main ingredient used in the Irish brew was barley, but with the introduction of the potato into Ireland in the early sixteenth century, they found it cheaper to use potatoes and sugar beet.

The mash was allowed to ferment, the starch would be turned into sugar, and the sugar would be turned into alcohol, and by evaporation and cooling, using a copper spiral worm in cold water, the poteen was produced. It was a slow and painstaking process.

They would set up the still in remote areas, well away from the interference and the prying eyes of the church and the state. Many of the clergy enjoyed a drop of poteen, whether it was for pleasure or medicinal purposes.

On the other hand, the church as a whole was very much against it, as it often resulted in drunk and disorderly behavior. Poteen was cheap and easy to make, and for many, it was all they could afford.

James and Tony could safely assume that the rising smoke from the still was not seen from the shore. Neither would the smoke from their campfire be seen as long as they stayed on the north side of the island facing away from the shore. They could feel quite safe lighting a fire without drawing attention.

That evening, they noticed some fish close to the shore and organized a net near the cabin. James set two or three snares at the rabbit burrows. They had not slept much in the last few days as they were afraid of nodding off and waking up to find themselves in the hands of the militia soldiers who seemed to be everywhere. They felt safe on this island with nobody around to disturb them. They could rest easy and catch up on their sleep. Here, they were able to relax and plan their next move.

Soon, they would have to return to the mainland and make contact with Father Pius, but for now it was time for relaxation and rest. The last thing they did before settling down for the night was to check the coastline for any sign of a boat.

The first thing they did in the morning was to check again for boats, even before they checked their net for fish. There was only one small fish in the net, but luckily, they had a few fish left over from the previous day. They sealed off a little pool where they could store some live fish for later. They lit their campfire and prepared and cooked two of the fish on a spit.

They would take a swim in the ocean later that day when the water might be warmer, but now, they would head into the interior to check the traps. The traps were empty, but there were definite signs of wildlife in the form of prints and droppings. Hopefully, they would have better luck tomorrow, declared Tony, trying not to sound too disappointed.

On their way back from exploring the island that morning, as they approached the cabin, they were surprised to see another boat pulled up on the beach. They had left plenty of evidence of their presence in the cabin. It was too late for a cover-up now. James remembered he had left the pistol in the cabin; in full sight where it could easily be found.

It did not take long before they saw a big, burly man accompanied by a boy come out of the cabin. The man was a typical fisherman with a big head of red hair and a thick red beard. He wore a homemade wool sweater, a tweed peaked hat, and a clay pipe, also called a 'dudeen' by the locals, hung out of the side of his mouth. The boy was about fourteen or fifteen, full of energy, checking here and there, and for what I do not know. The man carried two stoneware jugs out of the cabin and placed them in the boat.

James surmised that the jugs were likely full of poteen. It would be safe to say that the poteen was what brought him and the boy to the island in the first place. This island was where he had his still and where he stored his product. In all likelihood, he was getting ready for a poteen delivery for a wake or wedding. The man took a bag from the boat and left it in the cabin.

They left shortly after that and rowed back to the coast. The brothers watched them until they were well out of sight on their way back to the mainland.

The first thing they did was to check for the pistol. It was gone, and a bag of food was left behind in its place. Letting them know that the pistol had been found. He may have felt he was entitled to something of value for the use of his cabin.

The bag contained a cake of bread and some cheese. It was obviously left behind for them. The inference was that this fisherman was a friend, not a foe, but who was he? Will they ever know? If they ever met him again, they would certainly recognize that face.

James checked the stoneware jugs and found that most of them were full. He wondered why they were not worried about leaving all this stuff behind unprotected or if they were going to return with backup. Then Tony remembered Fr Pius and his warning from that first day, "Trust nobody" and "Do not mistake acts of kindness as acts of friendship."

James's first thought was the need to leave this island without delay. There was no easy escape; there was only one way off this island, and that window was closing fast; they had to leave tonight. They put their stuff back into the boat and headed for the mainland. It wasn't quite dark yet, but there was no time to waste. They could not let themselves be backed into a corner. They rowed back to the boathouse in record time.

They thought it would be safe there if only for a few hours to rest until it was dark enough to go see Fr Pius, that is if he was still willing to help them. When it got dark, they went to the church. The side door was unlocked; they waited for a while, but there was no sign of the priest. It was a cold night, so they lit a fire on the beach and waited the night out.

Bright and early the following morning, they returned to the church. Fr Pius was on the altar saying mass. They wanted to let him know they were back at the shore and needed his help. They waited for the collection plate to be passed around. They wrapped a gold ducat in a piece of cloth and placed it in the collection plate. They hoped that the gold would convey the right message.

Then Tony had a change of mind. Instead of the gold ducat, which might create suspicions if, by chance, it was discovered by the wrong person, he put the wooden rosary on the collection plate instead. He knew Fr Pius would recognize the beads and would be looking out for their arrival. In any case, they would have to wait and see what happens as they were running out of options.

When they got back within sight of the boathouse, there was a group of militia soldiers with sniffer dogs standing around, and readying a boat to go search the island. "The son of a bitch", mumbled Tony in Latin, his chosen language these days. "We should have burned down his cabin." They stayed well out of sight until the boat was on its way to the island. They would have to find somewhere else to hide.

They left the boathouse and went back to the church. It seemed like the only safe place to hide right now. They sneaked into the church through the side door. The church seemed deserted except for a few elderly ladies who were deep in prayer and meditation. They were aware that the church was the one place that the militia was likely to search, but not until they had checked out the island first.

They reckoned they had a few hours before anyone came looking, and hopefully, Fr Pius would turn up before then. The confessional box had three cubicles where people knelt to confess their sins in private, one for the priest in the center and one on each side for the laity. They both squeezed in as best they could into the priest's center cubicle. After a while, they realized that one of the ladies wanted to have her confession heard.

The brothers were familiar with the service, and did a very convincing job in Latin, and sent the lady away happy. A short time after, they had another and then another until they heard a commotion in the church. It was the militia soldiers looking for runaways.

The soldiers looked into the confessional cubicles on each side. Then Tony responded from behind the curtain by saying the sign of the cross in Latin as if getting ready to hear confession. *"Et nominee pater, et Filius, et spiteful sancta, et in sicula suculorum."*

That was convincing enough to the soldier, who recognized the prayer and responded with an apology and, indicating they were searching for Spanish escapees, and with that, they left the church. The brothers let out a sigh of relief while affirming their faith in the power of prayer. Tony had to hear three more confessions before Fr Pius came to investigate.

Pius had recognized the wooden rosary and was expecting Tony and his brother. He explained that he heard that the fisherman's wife gave their position away in return for the promise of money. However, he hadn't suspected that the runaways they were after were Tony and James, but now that they were here, he was happy to be of assistance in any way he could.

Fr Pius handed the brothers two Franciscan monk habits to wear. The hood covered their heads. And best of all, he had sandals to finish the ensemble. Fr Pius had put the word out among the parishioners that he was expecting some brother monks to visit from Rome to help him out in the parish. It was the perfect cover. They were not Spanish; they spoke Italian and Latin and were trained in the liturgy of the mass. They would fit right in until they had a plan to leave the country, and in the meantime, they could help out in the parish as deacons.

The role of the deacon, while not a priest, was to assist and administer to the physical needs of the church community, while the priest's job was to preach the word of God. The deacon was a person of honesty and sound character who would have the confidence of the people and would look after such activities as food programs for the poor and needy and cater to the unique needs of the parishioners.

Fr Pius brought them back to his home where they could relax and freshen up after having been on the run for days. After some nourishment and clean clothes, they recounted their experiences and what they witnessed since they last met.

They were shocked when Pius told them of all the ships that had run aground and were wrecked on the rocky west coast, driven ashore by the stormy weather and the terrible faith that awaited those sailors and soldiers as they struggled to make it to shore.

It was decided that it would be wise to keep a low profile for a few weeks or until all the excitement on the shore died down and all the spectators, speculators, and prospectors went home. In the meantime, like everything else in life, they would have to earn their keep and there was plenty to do in the Parish. Everything in the parish had fallen into disrepair because of cash shortages.

The church was in need of a new roof. The upkeep and everyday maintenance of the church required a lot of hard work. There was lots of poverty and hardship in the parish. Many people were struggling to make ends meet. James and Tony were not afraid of hard work. They welcomed the opportunity to be able to help out.

This was a farming community, and they were brought up on a farm after all. They were just happy to be able to walk around freely, if only for a short time. They were always afraid the wrong person might recognize them, so they kept to themselves as much as possible. They would always wear the habit when they were out in public.

In church one Sunday morning, they were helping Fr Pius with the service, greeting the parishioners and introducing themselves. Two men with very familiar faces came over to shake their hands; it was the 'de Marco' brothers, Carlos and Luigi. Carlos, not wanting to create a scene, whispered in Italian, "What have we got here, the captain's little pets."

When asked what they were doing there, Carlos responded in Italian that they had escaped to Scotland and were now soldiers of fortune enlisted with the O'Doherty Militia. Neither of them wanted any trouble and agreed to stay out of each other's way.

James told them of their suspicions as to who cut the foot rope, but they shrugged it off. "That could have been anybody. Why bother them with that shit." James and Tony were convinced that the 'de Marco' brothers were behind the attempt on their lives in revenge for what happened to their brother Jacques, but there was no proof, and not likely to be any. The best they could do now was to stay out of each other's way.

There was no trust between them, and likely never will be. The 'de Marco' brothers had a good cover in that they were not Spanish and were excellent soldiers with a wealth of fighting experience. James and Tony had the cover of the church, Fr Pius was their benefactor, they were not Spanish, but Italian spoke fluent Latin, were well versed in the church's liturgy, and were now accepted in the parish as men of God.

However, they must tell Fr Pius about their encounter with the 'de Marco 'brothers.

Chapter Fifteen
Catherine and Eileen

The months passed without incident, and James and Tony started to settle into their new life as part of the church community. They got more and more involved with the people. They were well-liked and went out of their way to be as helpful as possible. They were especially helpful in organizing and administering the charities in the parish. The bishop, who was aware of their situation, was very pleased to support Fr Pius in helping the two brothers and would do everything he could to help them make it back home to Venice.

The bishop had already made contact with Fr. Francesco back at the monastery to check out their stories. As a result, he and Francesco developed a friendship. This was a rural community, and the small farmers relied on their neighbors to help with the bigger jobs around the farm, like bringing in the harvest, saving the hay, trashing the corn, cutting the turf, and thatching the cottage roof. All of which took a community effort. James and Tony enjoyed working out in the fresh air. They were making some real friends and earning their keep in the process.

Many young men were lost at sea, trying to supplement their meager farming income. As a result, the parish always needed strong young men to help out with the heavy work on the land. Two ladies in particular lost their husbands in a fishing tragedy at sea the previous year. Catherine O'Reilly and Eileen O'Grady were two young widows struggling to manage their small farms on the other side of town. Both lost their husbands the night of the big storm.

The fleet was returning home, laden with a full catch of herring from the coast of Greenland, when they got caught in a hurricane. Their fishing boats broke up in the frigid waters of the North Atlantic among mountainous waves. The entire crew, their boats, and smacks were all lost that night. Masts, yards, and broken spars washed up on the shore for weeks afterwards.

The bodies of their husbands were never recovered from the sea. They checked the shoreline every day for any trace of the missing fishermen, but nothing ever turned up. Fr Pius was a great comfort to them in those times of grief, and they remained close friends ever since. The two ladies were friends all through their school years. They did everything together. They were both very active in the community and spent much of their time working with Fr. Pius for the church, especially in raising money to repair the church roof.

They organized bake sales and raffles, ran the soup kitchen for people in need, and were always on hand to help out when needed. They were lovely young ladies. Catherine was tall and handsome, with long black hair and beautiful brown eyes. Eileen was young and pretty with sparkling blue eyes and long blond hair. Both ladies were well known for their love of music, and both sang in the church choir.

With their consent, Pius volunteered the two brothers to help the ladies on the farm. The brothers, being experienced farmers, were happy to work out in the fresh air. The houses were small, with only one bedroom, so they slept in one of the outbuildings, which was common practice for farm laborers.

Their sleeping quarters were quite comfortable, clean, and way superior to what they were used to on the run. Of course, they would always join the ladies in the house at mealtime. The house was a typical thatched cottage with white-washed walls and a stone slab floor. The entrance had a split door or two half doors, so the top and bottom portions could be opened independently. The windows in the house were extra small, and when the weather allowed, it was normal for the upper portion of the door to be left open, allowing fresh air and daylight in while also keeping the free-range chickens and other farm animals out.

The front door opened straight into the kitchen with a bedroom to one side and a sitting room or parlor to the other. A small scullery or pantry was built as an extra room where food and vegetables were stored. The milk was separated and churned to make butter and cheese in what was called the dairy, a small room next to the pantry.

As was common in the area, every house had a bog or a piece of bog land property that went with the house. Turf was the primary fuel used for burning, with the odd wooden log from trees chopped down around the ditches on the farm. Every summer, the men would spend a week or two cutting the turf and laying it out on the ground to dry. When dry, the turf would be drawn home in creels, which were large woven wicker baskets carried on a donkey's back and stored as a rick or stack close to the house.

The best thing about turf was it was cheap, and there was plenty of it. The kitchen had an open-hearth fireplace where all the cooking took place. The fire hearth had iron hooks that could swing back and forth to accommodate large pots, kettles, baking trays, and cauldrons of hot water over the blazing fire. The house was always warm, and there was always something cooking. The smell of homemade bread fresh off the Griddle always filled the air. Then again, the aroma of a big pot of Irish Stew might fill your nostrils.

The teapot was always on the brew, and the homemade scones, with butter and homemade strawberry jam, were always on hand. There were always two comfortable chairs in front of the fire and, at least one being a rocking chair, maybe two. A large table in the middle of the floor and a dresser with rows of dishes on display. An old-fashioned clock, a spinning wheel, and an oil lamp for night use only.

A statue of Our Lady, the Child of Prague, and a picture of the Sacred Heart adorned the mantle over the fireplace. There was an outhouse or washroom facility. Laundry had to be done by hand using an aluminum tub and a washing board. There was an even larger aluminum bathtub that could be filled with hot water from the cauldron for personal use. There was always hot water heating over the fire. Fresh water was carried from the well close to the house and was used for both the animals and the household.

There were several outbuildings for housing animals, milking cows, and storing grain, as well as a workshop for housing and repairing farm tools and equipment.

The brothers worked hard alongside the ladies on the farm. Feeding and watering the animals, mending fences and digging ditches, chopping wood, picking potatoes, and saving the hay. There was lots of work to keep them busy. The brothers planted a vegetable garden in their spare time close to the house that supplied all the vegetables they needed. They all got along well despite the language barrier.

The women spoke Gaelic as a first language. They were not fluent in English, knowing just enough to get by. James and Tony were well aware of what needed to be done around the farm and did not need much direction from the ladies, and before long, they got into their own routine. The women were always around to help. The brothers learned to speak a little Gaelic and became more fluent daily.

It was inevitable as they were spending so much time in each other's company, they developed feelings for each other and grew closer together. Even though they were introduced as monks, Fr Pius had explained that although they were raised in a monastery, they had never taken a vow of chastity or made any other commitment to the church. Still, he would not like that to be common knowledge among the parishioners who considered them as men of God.

The women had not felt safe on their own since their husbands drowned, and when the crowds of treasure seekers were pouring into the neighborhood, they had frequent robberies and break-ins. Fences were broken, and chickens and eggs were stolen. The brothers grinned as they thought this was very understandable, with so many sailors like themselves on the run. Now that James and Tony were around, the women no longer had any reason to fear.

It was also noticed from watching the brothers working shirtless in the fields in the hot summer sun they were very handsome young men; they were fit and well-built. They were young, strong, smart, and knowledgeable, with many skillsets. They were good farmers, and most of all, in the lady's eyes, they were available.

As it turned out, the ladies loved to play music, especially Irish Ceilidh music and dance. They liked to tell stories of leprechauns and fairies, banshees and goblins, and ancient warriors like 'Oisin', 'Finn McCool' and

'Cuchulainn'. They both sang like the nightingale and were in the church choir.

James and Tony impressed the ladies with their singing voices and liked to sing along despite the language difference. They liked to sing their shanties to the lady's amusement while working in the hot sun. They developed a taste for buttermilk to quench their thirst and were quite at home on the farm. When the ladies found out that the brothers liked music and singing, it didn't take long before they organized a party in the house or an Irish ceilidh, as the locals called it.

The musical instruments were taken down and dusted, the neighbors, friends, and family were invited, and the seanachai, the local storyteller, was also there. The floor was cleared, and the food was prepared. Seamus Mac Callan arrived with his son Thigh to deliver a stoneware jug of his finest poteen and a barrel of homemade beer. It would not be a proper party without an ample supply of beer or poteen.

Both James and Tony recognized their bearded fisherman friend and his son immediately. They would like to ask for their pistol back, but that was a memory better left back on the Island. This was the brothers' first exposure to Celtic music, song, and dance. They were very taken by the sound of the Irish fiddle and the bodhran. They picked up the rhythm fast, and in no time, they were leading the ladies around the floor.

That night, they realized that they had a lot in common with Catherine and Eileen. They were fun to be around, and wished this night would never end. They spent many happy hours together, and in time, the women got over their grief, and the brothers settled down to a normal existence, not always looking over their shoulders. They started to pick up the language, and every day, they would learn a few words in both Gaelic and English. They had always found it easy to pick up a new language.

The big incentive was being able to communicate with Catherine and Eileen. They concluded that the Gaelic speakers were predominately Irish Catholic and the English speakers were predominately protestant and loyal to the Crown.

As time passed, the brothers became more and more part of the community. They grew closer to Catherine and Eileen and no longer slept in the outbuilding. It would be safe to say that love was definitely in the air. In the evening, all four liked to ramble along the country lanes with the stone walls on each side, covered with blackberry bushes that divided the small farm holdings. They would stop and chat and say hello to their neighbors or walk along the seashore and watch the waves roll in. See the puffins and the seagulls diving, competing for fish, or watch the seals dive deep after the salmon.

On a clear day, they could make out the fishing boats with the wind at their back, heading leeward out into the North Atlantic to the fishing grounds of Greenland in search of the sholes of cod and herring. When the tide was out, they would wade out into the cool salty water, avoiding the crabs and the jellyfish, or walk along the rocky shore collecting mussels and periwinkles, or just collect shells on the sandy beach.

None of them could refrain from inspecting every little object they saw in the sand that might connect with the past and remind them of loved ones and friends they lost to the sea. Sometimes, while working in the fields, the ladies would spread a picnic under the shade of the old oak tree by the stream, where they would while away an hour or two in the hot summer afternoon, and the men would quench their thirst on a cold jug of beer or buttermilk.

Tony was still harboring aspirations of entering the church. He believed that his experiences on the 'Trinidad Valencera' had strengthened his resolve and vocation for the priesthood. He saw it as his true calling. He felt the time was right, and the sooner he left, the better for all concerned. They got to know a few fishermen around the area and became familiar with some ship owners who sailed over and back to Scotland. He was told he could work his passage. They were always looking for able-bodied seamen with experience.

Now that the English were no longer looking for Spanish survivors, he felt it was safe to make his way back to Francesco and the monastery. If only he could reach the French coast, he was confident he could make it home to Venice from there. He hated leaving Eileen behind, but he knew he had to give the priesthood a try. He had never thought that strongly about family life. He wasn't even sure if it would work out in the long run.

Eileen was a very beautiful woman and would have no trouble getting any man she wanted. Maybe this was just a flirtation, and the feelings would pass with time. Did he want to grow old in this land where he had no roots, didn't speak the language, and the only real friends he had were Fr Pius and James? What if James goes to sea and the aging Fr Pius dies? What then?

He had talked it through with Eileen and James. Eileen would not stand in his way if that was what he wanted. James was deeply in love with Catherine, but he was not sure what he wanted. He was staying put for now; he was not sure if this was where his future lay, but he didn't see his future back in the monastery with Francesco.

One afternoon, the four of them borrowed a boat and went back over to the island. The ladies packed a picnic basket and some home-baked goods. They were surprised at how well the two men knew their way around the Island. They were even more surprised when they produced a stoneware jar of alcohol from the shack. This was a sort of pilgrimage for James and Tony.

They lit a fire on the sandy beach, cooked some fish, and enjoyed some delicious food together. They swam in the ocean, dried off, and lay in the hot sun. They picked some mussels on the shore and strolled along the beach with the ladies before they ventured inland. They finally came to the big chestnut tree in the middle of the clearing.

While the ladies were busy elsewhere, the brothers retrieved the tin box, which was all charred and covered in black soot. They figured what happened was that day when the militia were searching for them on the island. They must have gathered under the chestnut tree, where they sheltered from the rain. They would have lit a fire to keep warm or to heat some food and did not realize they were literally sitting on a gold mine.

James and Tony wrapped the box up in a coat and brought it with them. They sat on the beach until it was getting dark and then headed back to the mainland.

That night, Tony packed the crucifix and the rosary into his backpack. He would bring them back to Venice, and Francesco would know what to do with them. They should be in a church anyway. He left the gold coins with James to do whatever he wanted with them. He said they brought nothing but bad luck to those who had them. Maybe James could put them to better use.

They all went to see Fr Pius, and Tony thanked him for being such a good friend and said his goodbyes. It was two days after that Tony hugged Eileen one last time. James was also sad to see him go but tried not to let it show for Eileen's sake. In any case, he was happy for Tony if this was what he really wanted.

However, having been through so much together, he felt very empty inside. He threw his arms around his brother and feared he would never see him again. They all watched Tony get into the boat to be rowed out to the ship waiting in the bay. They watched as the ship hauled up the anchor, and the breeze filled her sail. They stayed until she moved out beyond the harbor wall on her way to Scotland.

Chapter Sixteen
The Mary Rose

James did not want to keep the gold coins in the house and was looking for a place around the farm to hide them. One day, he was looking at the sky when he noticed a rainbow. When he looked closer, it appeared that one end of the rainbow was right at the top of the big oak tree by the river. This was the tree Catherine and Eileen liked to sit under, where all four of them had so many pleasant evenings together, picnicking in the warm summer sun. This was where he decided to hide the gold at the end of the rainbow.

He put it all in a tin box and wrapped it well before he buried it at the base of the tree and covered it with stones. It would be safe there until it was needed. The last thing they wanted was to be seen flashing money about. He did not want to draw attention to himself or Catherine. This pot of gold would be safe for the time being under the old oak tree.

Word was getting around that the 'de Marco' brothers were spending a lot of time in the 'Thatch', the local alehouse in the village. They were well known for spending money and buying drinks for the locals, and you might say they were everybody's best friend, especially the owner 'Fergus Muldoon'.

Tony found himself in Glasgow, Scotland, the next day. Glasgow was a small provincial market town that traded with Ireland, England, France, the

Baltic, the Netherlands, and, of course, the rest of Scotland. He got a room near the waterfront and got a job loading and unloading ships in an effort to earn enough to get to Venice.

One day, after unloading a French ship, the captain offered to let him work his way back to France. When he reached France, he had no trouble getting a boat back to Venice. When he reached Venice, the first thing he did was to look up Maria and Rosa.

He was surprised to find that they were both married and settled down. He had not expected them to wait for his return but felt obliged to explain why they did not make it back, reassure them that it was out of their control, and tell them the whole fascinating, if unbelievable, story.

He stayed the night with Michael Simone before continuing to meet with Francesco at the monastery. Michael told him that the news of the Balanzera and the tragedy that befell her and her crew had already arrived in Venice. There were no Venetian survivors that they knew of.

As they walked through the park that evening, Tony told Michael all the details of his voyage to Sicily, the requisitioning of the Balanzara by the Spanish, the battle of Gravelines, the North Sea voyage, the Shipwreck on Inishowen, the massacre at Elagh Castle, rescue by Fr Pius and how he and James met Catherine and Eileen. He knew that Michael met many sailors through his guesthouse and was very involved and keenly interested in the maritime history of Venice.

He passed on the letters he had been entrusted with, and Michael promised to see that they would be delivered through his maritime historical society. It was also important to Tony that the atrocities and murders at Elagh be made public to the civilized world, and Michael was just the person to do that.

The following morning, Tony set out bright and early for the monastery in the mountains. The local people were very friendly and accommodating along the road. He could not help feeling happy to be on his way home despite the sadness of leaving Eileen and James behind in Inishowen.

Francesco came out to meet him with open arms when he reached the monastery. They had so many stories to tell and so much catching up to do. Tony could not wait to tell Francesco his incredible story of how he had come to have the crucifix and rosary and handed them to him. Francesco agreed they should be either in a museum or the gold cross with the relic of St Francis of Assisi, which should be retained for safekeeping in the monastery. He had all the information and would consult with Rome about what should be done.

Tony told Francesco of his desire to join the priesthood. He told him of all the time he spent with the sick and dying and how he felt about that. How he often thought of becoming a priest and believed that was what he was meant to do. Francesco agreed to prepare him for the priesthood at the monastery under his supervision. Tony was more than qualified, and with Fr. Francesco as his sponsor, all he needed was the blessing of a bishop.

As the months passed back in Inishowen, James was feeling more and more at home with Catherine on the farm. He had moved into the cottage, but he was struggling with the notion of settling down with Catherine for life or answering the call of the sea. He was overjoyed when Catherine told him she was pregnant. That helped make up his mind. However, Catherine always had trouble with childbirth and had never been able to hold on to a baby. She had miscarriage after miscarriage in the past, and while the doctor had not ruled out a child in the future, advised her to give up trying for a few years at least to give her body a chance to recover. They were so happy with the thought of having their child that they both hoped for the best.

On the one hand, he still dreamed of sailing the oceans and visiting exotic lands and places on the other side of the world, but on the other hand, he loved Catherine and promised he would stand by her no matter what. Catherine wondered if James would ever be happy as she often watched him staring out to the sea as he strolled along the shore, watching the waves roll in from the Atlantic.

Would he always be the foreigner, the stranger in a strange land, a fish out of water, a square peg in a round hole? Before she was pregnant, she always wondered if James was happy in Inishowen. Would he be like Tony and get up and leave someday? What was there to keep him here, especially now that Tony was gone? Now, however, things were different. They were going to be a real family. They were so happy together so in love.

James often thought to himself that divine providence brought them to this rocky shore, rescued them from the cruel sea, and made him witness to the atrocities and greed of his fellow man. Where he met Catherine, this place was his only real home, a place where he could spend the rest of his life. He loved Catherine with all his heart and could not bear to leave her or their baby.

It all came to a head one day. James was out in the field looking after the sheep. The 'de Marco' brothers, Carlos and Luigi, came around looking for mischief. They arrived at Catherine's cottage, where she was home alone. They had been drinking all morning in the 'Thatch'. First, they asked where James was and when he was expected back. She told them he should be along shortly, and then they asked for a drink of water as it was a hot day.

When she went to get it, they followed her into the house. She protested, but they forced their way in anyway. When she told them to get out, they demanded to know where James had hidden his gold. When they saw she had no knowledge of any gold, Carlos said she shouldn't be so shy and asked her for a little kiss. When she refused, he got abusive and accused her of being a slut, pushing her to the ground and tore open her dress. Carlos was the first to take advantage, forcing himself on her. When he was done,

Luigi took his turn. Catherine pleaded, but all she could hear was their laughter ringing in her ear. They finally left, laughing and shouting as they headed back to the village.

A neighbor who heard the commotion rushed over to the cottage. Catherine made it to the front door to call for help, and that is where they found her. She was battered and bruised, and blood flowing down her legs. Eileen arrived to see what was happening, having heard the laughs and shouts of the drunk 'de Marco' brothers going down the lane on their way back to the village. James had just returned from looking after the sheep and rushed to see what was all the commotion when he saw the people gathered at the house. Eileen and James carried Catherine inside and laid her on the bed. It did not take long before a miscarriage was confirmed.

When James heard the full story of what had transpired in his absence, he could hardly believe his ears. The temper and rage grew inside him until he could no longer control his anger. He grabbed an iron rod from the hearth and headed for the village. His first stop was the 'Thatch', and it wasn't a drink he was after.

Carlos and Luigi were standing and drinking at the bar. Their glasses were full, and they were having a laugh. Probably joking about how they taught Catherine O'Reilly a lesson she would not forget in a hurry. James was now moving with the lightning speed of a matador going in for the kill.

He smashed the glasses of beer in front of the two men with the iron rod. The shattered glass and beer went flying everywhere. Carlos and Luigi, who had been drinking all day, were caught by surprise, and for a moment, amid the flying glass, splattered beer, and crashing noise, they were totally dazed.

Both of them had blood mixed with beer flowing down their faces from the shattered glass. They tried to say something in their drunken state, but James had no time for small talk. Carlos took out his dagger, the same one he got from Jacques, and threw it at James, missing its mark. He then fired his pistol, missing James by inches. James whipped him across his knees with the iron bar and watched him fall to the ground, yelling in agony.

As he hit the ground, he knocked his head hard on the metal foot rail. He did not get back up. James smashed a stool across his back, making sure he stayed down. Luigi had drawn his pistol and was waving it about, trying to steady his aim in his drunken state. When he finally got off a shot, James saw the flash in the pan and was already moving.

The pistol fired and grazed him in the left shoulder. Before Luigi could reload, James picked up Carlos's dagger and threw it with his right hand, lodging it squarely in Luigi's chest. James broke two more stools before he walked out of that pub, with neither of the 'de Marco' brothers moving.

James was still in a rage when he got back to the house. Catherine was still in a state of shock when he got home but a little more relaxed from her ordeal. He fell to his knees and cried for having left her alone in her condition, for letting such a thing happen; he would never forgive himself. He brought her nothing but trouble ever since he first came into her life. It was one thing after another.

Eileen disinfected and bandaged James's wounds, which were superficial and non-life threatening, nothing more than a skin graze. An hour or two passed as they reflected on everything that happened that day. James declared that the 'de Marcos' had it coming. They deserved everything they got and a lot worse.

Soon after, they heard a horse coming up the lane. It was Johnny Mac Namara, otherwise known as Johnny Mac, a good friend and neighbor of Catherine's. He brought news from the village. Luigi died from the knife wound to the chest, and Carlos was in a coma and was being treated for a head injury. He was not expected to last the night.

The barman, Fergus Muldoon, had protested their innocence, saying his customers were having a quiet drink when they were maliciously attacked by James. Now, the police were on their way to arrest James, who knew that his chances of getting a fair trial were slim to non-existent. He would have to get out of the country and fast, at least until tempers cooled down and he could tell his side of the story. Catherine agreed; she knew he would likely be hanged if caught.

Johnny Mac had news of a ship, 'The Mary Rose', that was waiting in the bay, ready to sail with the tide. The owner's name was Malcolm Macpherson; he was no friend of the Crown but a good friend of Johnny Mac, someone he would trust with his life. He could get James passage to Scotland that night, and from there, he could make his way back home to Italy.

James did not want to leave Catherine in her condition, but she was well-loved and had many friends in the community she could turn to for help. He had brought her nothing but trouble, and he believed that this was the best way out for all concerned. He packed a few things in a sack, but before he left, he took what remained of the gold coins and placed them into Catherine's hands.

He told her where the gold coins came from and how they were in his possession. Fr Pius could tell her the rest of the story. He told her to do whatever she thought best with the gold. He said, "Put it to good use; many good men had died for it". He told her what Tony had said before he left and how they were on the 'Trinidad Valencera' crew. He kissed her and promised he would be back. He said he would never forget her as he headed out the front door into the black night.

By the time the police came looking for James, the 'Mary Rose' had long sailed. Catherine and Eileen made statements, but they did not get much sympathy from the police. Catherine felt that James had avenged her terrible ordeal, but there was nothing one could say or do that would erase that terrible memory or make up for the loss of her baby and a true friend that was nowhere to be found now.

Catherine hid the gold in the same place under the old oak tree as James suggested and wondered what she would do with all that gold. She kept thinking what James had said about putting it to good use, that many good men had died for it. She had not told Eileen about it but felt that as Tony's partner, she also should have a say.

Time went by. Summer turned into Fall, and Fall turned into Spring. The birds were back singing on the porch. Buds were starting to appear on the trees. Snowdrops and daffodils started to blanket the landscape. The thorny gorse and the whin bushes, characteristic of the Atlantic coastal heathland and montane habitat, began to blossom in abundance with their beautiful yellow foliage and distinctive coconut cent. Signs of a new life were everywhere, with the lambs playing in the fields and the birds busy building their nests.

While James and Tony were less and less spoken about, they were not forgotten. Catherine and Eileen were resigned to the possibility that they might never see them again. Some of the men from the village started to show up around the farm with a keen interest in Catherine and Eileen. Catherine knew Eileen had been seeing other men and was not over-surprised when Eileen started to show. She asked her once but did not get a straight answer.

It was a bright sunny morning that March when Eileen gave birth to a bouncing baby boy. Seven pounds eight ounces, blue eyes, sallow skin, and a big head of red hair. Catherine did not ask who the father was, and nobody really cared. If Eileen wanted to say, she would in her own good time. It was not an easy birth, and Eileen took a while to get back on her feet even though she did not fully recover. She suffered from fatigue and depression.

Catherine was always at her side to help when needed. Both women doted over the baby, who did not want for anything. In the tradition of the Catholic Church, the child had to be blessed and christened with oil and holy water. They were all gathered in the church, and Fr Pius performed the service. When he asked, "What name will he be called?". Eileen's reply was, "Call him after his father, Anthony Gallen." Both Fr Pius and Catherine nodded in agreement and agreed it was a very nice name without showing their utmost surprise.

"This would change everything," thought Fr Pius and Catherine. "Tony needed to know. They would have to get word to him somehow, whether Eileen wanted it or not." Fr Pius knew the bishop had been in contact with Fr. Francesco and could send a message faster using the papal courier.

Meanwhile, they would bide their time and see what developed. As for Catherine, she had made up her mind that Eileen had a say in what happened to the gold coins. She would have to confide with Eileen, tell her the whole story, and put things right. Fr Pius told the bishop about the revelation of Tony's child and suggested he should relay the news of the birth to Francesco.

When Francesco received the news from the Bishop and Fr. Pius, his first thoughts were of happiness and joy at the birth of a grandson. He was so happy he rushed to tell Anthony. When Francesco conveyed the news to Anthony, he saw that he was overjoyed but also saddened that he was not there with her. He left her when she needed him most for his own selfish desire to be a priest. He had to go to her to put things right. He needed to be with his wife and son.

Francesco knew of Tony's strong aspirations to join the church but had to advise him that he had always wished for one or both of them to be priests, but if God had taken them halfway around the world and kept them alive in spite of all they had been through, then that is where he wanted them to be.

Tony was still overwhelmed by the news. If only he knew, he would never have left her. He was so wrapped up in what he wanted himself. Will she ever forgive him? He must go back. He must go back now. Francesco looked at him as a father and felt his pain. He knew Tony would do the right thing.

One way or the other, he had to go back and see his child. He had to go back and talk it through with Eileen. He owed her that much.

Chapter Seventeen

Glasgow

Tony spent the week with his uncle before taking a ship out of Venice for the French coast. From there, he worked his passage all the way up to Scotland and arrived in Glasgow a few days later. He made his way to the harbor front and inquired about a ship to carry him over to Ireland. He was directed to an alehouse on the dockside where they were always looking for sailors.

The alehouse was packed with seamen, some looking for work, some looking for women, and some there just for the beer. He could hardly find his way around the dark and smoky alehouse. He sat down in a corner and ordered a beer. When the landlady finally brought it, he inquired if she knew of any ships going to Ireland. She said she would ask around, and if she heard ought, she would let him know. Finally, a voice he knew came billowing through the smoke and the noise of the crowd. "So, it's Inishowen, you are headed to, you have come to the right place. Can you pay, or are you looking for a free ride"?

That was the one voice he thought he would never hear again. A voice he knew so well ever since he was a boy. Out of the smoke stepped James like a ghost appearing out of the mist. They threw their arms around each other, with utter disbelief at what had just transpired in this back street bar on the docks of Glasgow. "What are you doing here, you son of a gun?

Where did you come from, how did you get here, who sent you?" James had so many questions.

Tony was able to fill James in on all that had happened back in Inishowen. James brought Tony home to his own place, where they spent the night making plans together, just like old times. James had stayed on with Malcolm Macpherson and the 'Mary Rose' as first mate. Macpherson found James to be a man he could trust and respect. James had proved himself worthy of Malcolm's trust and friendship on more than one occasion over their months together. He had risked life and limb in all types of stormy weather to protect both cargo and passengers from ruin and disaster.

They became very close friends and trusted each other emphatically. Malcolm's health was failing, and he found he had to rely more and more on James. He finally decided to retire and made James the captain of the Mary Rose.

Anthony was also able to advise James that Fr. Pius had spoken with the barman of the 'Thatch', Fergus Muldoon, and told him the danger of giving false evidence to the police. Fergus revised his statement to admit it was a case of self-defense as James was unarmed, and the 'de Marco' brothers had both discharged their pistols that night.

The Militia were more embarrassed than anything else to find out that both Carlos and Luigi were both seamen with the Armada. The 'Lord

Deputy' in Dublin, William Fitzwilliam, had ordered the capture and execution of all Armada soldiers, notwithstanding the fact that both the 'de Marco' brothers were guilty of rape. As a result, all charges against James were dropped. On hearing this, James decided it was time to go home.

In the meantime, back home in Ireland, Catherine told Eileen the full story of how the two brothers got to be in Inishowen. What they endured as crew members on the 'Trinidad Valencera'. The battle of Gravelines, the storms they encountered, and the treachery and hardship they endured on their voyage around Scotland. Their capture and treatment at the hands of the O'Doherty militia soldiers and their escape and rescue by Fr Pius. James and Tony had not told Fr Pius about the gold, fearing that it might implicate him in their escape.

Now Catherine and Eileen both felt it was time to sit down with Fr Pius and tell him what they knew and hear what he had to say. He concluded that the gold was not stolen; the brothers came about it legally. While some of it may be questionable, none was illegal in God's eyes. They decided that it should be put to good use, as was the wishes of James and Tony.

The church roof needed to be fixed. Anthony's baby was entitled, and Catherine should have a share. The decision was made. First, they would fix the church roof and split the remainder three ways. That was what was decided, and that was what they all agreed. It was assumed that most of it, if not all, would be used to help the community in any case.

One day, soon after that, the Mary Rose showed up in the bay. The captain and some of the crew came ashore in a small boat. They made their way up to the village. When Catherine opened the door and saw James standing there, she could not believe her eyes. She was lost for words. She broke down and cried as she hugged and kissed him and whispered, "I love you". James grabbed her with both arms and told her he was back to stay if she would have him. She replied, with tears of joy still in her eyes, "Yes, I will, Yes I will". She held him close and kissed him again and again and said, "I am so glad you came back."

He explained how he met up with the ship's owner, who asked him to captain his ship. The ship ferries people and cattle and whatever else between Ireland and Scotland. Two trips every month during the winter and a return trip every week in the summer. The promise of a partnership if all goes well. I get to do what I want in life and be with the woman I love.

James wanted to sail and find hidden treasure. Well, he did just that. In his mind, Catherine O'Reilly was his hidden treasure, and no money could buy that. He told her he had also brought a passenger, who was over checking out his new son. Tony had come home with him. When Fr Pius sent word to Venice, Tony decided that this was where he ought to be, with his wife and son.

Catherine and James hurried over to Eileen's house, where Fr Pius was also waiting to perform the marriage ritual. James and Catherine asked if they could make it a double wedding, and that was what they did. Fr Pius made the announcement. "This wedding is long overdue. Let's not waste any more time; the celebrations can wait."

James and Catherine and Tony and Eileen made their marriage vows, and Fr Pius blessed them all in holy matrimony. James presented a jug of wine and called for a toast 'to good friends and family. May they always find their way back home.'

Life was good that summer and the two families settled down. Tony could not wait for his son to grow up. There was so much he had to teach him. Eileen never recovered fully after the birth of her son. Her immune system was weak, and she came down with every virus that came her way.

In the fall of that year, she got a fever and could not shake it. It was two weeks after Christmas when she passed away. Tony was heartbroken and inconsolable, and Catherine and James looked after their son. It was in late January when Catherine was alone in the house, and a knock came to the door. James was out looking after the animals. The stranger introduced himself as Jacques de Marco.

He pushed his way into the house and said, "I believe you know my brothers Carlos and Luigi. Well, I am here to even the score, as the bible says, 'an eye for an eye, don't you agree, young lady.' He took something of mine, and now I want something of his in return. And that just might be you, where about is he?". Just then, they could hear James's voice outside in the yard. He was back from the fields.

Jacques grabbed Catherine, and held his dagger to her throat, and took out his pistol. When James came through the door and came face to face with Jacques de Marco, he could not believe his eyes. He thought he had seen the last of him. Jacques explained that his friends had paid off his jailers.

"Everyone has their price, and what is yours for me to make this easy on you. How much gold is she worth?" The words were barely out of his mouth when Tony walked into the kitchen, followed by Fr Pius. Catherine bit his hand, making him release his grip. He threw her to one side, and James made a move.

Jacques aimed his pistol at James, and as it went off, Fr Pius stepped in front of James, taking the bullet in the chest. Catherine was now on her feet, rushing to the defense of her husband. She grabbed a log from the fireplace and struck Jacques hard on the side of the head. Jacques slumped to the ground and never got up. They laid Fr Pius on the bed and sent for a medic.

James and Tony tried to stop the bleeding, but the gunshot was at close range, and the wound was fatal. Pius died before the medic arrived. They mourned the loss of a true friend they loved and regarded as part of their family.

They buried Fr Pius beside Eileen's grave underneath the willow overlooking the North Atlantic Ocean. It was Tony's idea. It was where he wanted to be himself when his time came. He liked to go there with his son Anthony; they would sit there by her grave looking out to the sea, and he would tell his son all about Venice and life in the Alps, how he and James climbed mountains together, and their adventures on the 'Trinidad Valencera'.

After Eileen's death, Tony did not want to remarry; Eileen's people took over and worked the farm. James and Catherine reared Anthony Junior. Tony was thinking of the priesthood again. He spoke to the bishop, who spoke to Francesco, and they both agreed that he was ready to take over the Parish now that Fr Pius was no longer around.

A date was set for his ordination, and everyone was invited. The bishop, the Abbot, and the whole Franciscan community of monks were there. The church was packed with all of their neighbors and friends. A ship sailed into the bay that day, and a horse and trap were laid on for the arrival of one more guest. When he walked into the church that day in the middle of the ceremony, the bishop stopped the service to announce the arrival of Fr. Francesco all the way from Venice, Italy, and introduced him to the congregation. There was no need to introduce him to James, who turned to his wife and said, "Catherine, meet my father." "Anthony Junior, say hello. This is your granddad."

Fr. Francesco was on the altar when Fr. Anthony said his first mass, and during the mass, he handed a wooden case to Anthony containing the battered gold cross with the relic of Saint Francis of Assisi. It was with the permission and the blessing of the holy father that the cross should continue in the care of Fr. Anthony, who took care of it on its voyage to Inishowen.

That voyage is not yet finished. The cross and relic of Saint Francis of Assisi are being left in the care of Fr. Anthony himself and not the church, which is going through a trying time in the middle of King Henry VIII's Protestant Reformation.

Epilogue - The End of the Beginning

After King Henry's divorce and his marriage to Ann Boleyn was rejected by the Catholic Church, religion became a major cause of strife and division in Ireland, and Inishowen was no exception. The Crown demanded allegiance from the local chieftains and required that the Catholic Church be Anglicized under the control of the Church of English.

Monasteries were dissolved, and the extensive church lands were taken and given to those loyal to the Crown. Under the new system, local Chieftains were given land and titles by surrendering their lands as sovereign chieftains under the ancient Celtic Order and having them regranted to them as tenants of the Crown.

During the latter part of the 16th century 'Hugh O'Neill' succeeded Shane O'Neill as the Chieftain of the O'Neill clan in Co. Tyrone, a neighboring county to Donegal, governed by the O'Donnell chieftains. His grandfather 'Conn O'Neill', was previously granted the title of 'Earl of Tyrone' by Queen Elizabeth on the submission and regranting of his land. Hugh succeeded his grandfather as the 2nd earl of Tyrone and, at one time, was a staunch ally of the Crown. He was brought up as a protestant by an English foster family and was fluent in the English language.

However, 'Hugh O'Neill' had the bigger ambition of becoming the undisputed leader of all Ulster with the help of the other Irish Chieftains who had no love for the Crown. Having turned against the Crown by attacking the English fort on the Blackwater River, Hugh O'Neill made alliances with some of the most important Irish Celtic Families in Ulster, to the displeasure of Queen Elizabeth. The two biggest powers in Ulster were now the O'Donnell's of Tirconnell, in Donegal, and the O'Neill's of Tyrone. Together, they won many guerrilla skirmishes and battles against the forces of the Crown.

Feelings of patriotism ran high among the native Irish, who were essentially Roman Catholic and, as such, were opposed to the Reformation and the English occupation of Ireland. Many of the young men rallied to the cause and took up arms supporting O'Neill and O'Donnell. There were many skirmishes and gun battles between the Crown and the Irish Rebels.

James and Tony tried to avoid any direct involvement in the conflict but felt sympathetic to the Irish cause on both the religious and political front. Having witnessed the murders at Elagh Castle, they had no reservation as to what side they were on. When the troubles erupted closer to home, the local men took up arms on one side or the other.

An air of secrecy and suspicion spread throughout the community. Traitors and informants were executed on both sides. One Saturday night, a group of Irish rebels raided a military barracks in the area. They were looking for weapons and ammunition. Their plan was leaked by an informer to the garrison defending the barracks, and the militia were ready and waiting to spring the trap.

A battle ensued, and several men were shot and killed that night. A pistol bearing the initials C J C on the stock ('Captain James Cook') was left behind by one of the rebels, which was traced back to an earlier murder at Burt Castle. Items found at that murder scene, two muskets, and two army uniforms were linked to two more murders at Elagh Castle. A search party was organized for rebels on the run.

One man was described as a biggish man with red hair and a red beard. If caught, they would most definitely be facing the death penalty. Fergus Muldoon, the innkeeper of the 'Thatch,' was one of four rebels shot dead that night. When James heard the news, he knew precisely who two of the rebels were. He also had a good idea where they were hiding. They were Seamus Mac Callan and his son Thigh Mac Callan, the beer masters. Seamus was a good friend of Catherine's, and James felt obliged to help him escape the country.

It was late that night when a boat pulled into the little cove between the cliffs on the north side of the island. Some food was left in the shack with a message written in the Irish language: 'I will be waiting by the light of the silvery moon. Signed: Your darling Mary Rose'. James recognized the boat as it emerged from the mist, and three men were welcomed aboard the Mary Rose. The police had been checking all boats in and out of the harbor that day.

They checked every passenger and every cargo shipment coming and leaving the shore. They never suspected anyone being picked up from the far side of the island. A crown official came aboard for a final inspection before the Mary Rose set sail that night. The rebels were safely hidden in a secret compartment on the 'Mary Rose' that was only accessible through a trapdoor in the captain's cabin. James had it installed when he took over as captain of the ship. You never know when you might need such a place.

James used to refer to this secret compartment as the 'Chestnut Tree.' Seamus had originally immigrated from Scotland when he was young to follow his young bride, Mary-Ann McGinty, to Inishowen. Mary-Ann and Seamus were good friends of Catherine's and were always there to help when times got tough after the death of her husband. Seamus had lots of relatives in Scotland and would be quiet at home there.

The escape route to Scotland was well-defined. The first stage was organized by Johnny Mac, a well-known and trusted friend of Catherine and someone well known and trusted in the community. Rebels on the run from the Crown would row their boat to the far side of the Island where they would stay out of sight, hidden from the authorities until it was safe to meet up with the 'Mary Rose' and slip away to Scotland in the quiet hours of the night.

Seamus Mac Callan and his friends would meet and care for them on the other side. Seamus wanted his wife Mary-Ann to follow him when it was safe to do so. The authorities were watching his house day and night, expecting Seamus to show up sooner or later. When asked where Seamus was, Mary-Ann told them that he went fishing and never returned.

One stormy night, his boat was washed up on the shore. It was badly broken up and pretty weather-beaten, suggesting it was adrift in the North Atlantic Ocean for some time. However, there was no sign of Seamus or his son Thigh. The authorities stopped watching his house after that. The whole community grieved the drowning death of Seamus and his son. In her grief, Mary-Ann decided to go live with a friend in Scotland.

It was sometime after Mary-Ann was reunited with her husband. Seamus asked James if he could bring his distilling equipment, including the still and his earthenware jars, over to Scotland to continue producing the product, which he called it, for the Irish market in Inishowen. James could ship the product back to Inishowen on a regular basis. He was willing to pay him handsomely for his part in this business venture, as he put it.

Fergus Muldoon's wife, Nula, was heartbroken after the death of her husband. She lost all interest in the 'Thatch', and when it started to go downhill, she put it up for sale. James, who spent most of his time at sea, did not have the time to run the farm, and Catherine was not able to handle it on her own. After discussing the situation with Catherine, they decided to give up the farm and take over the running of the 'Thatch' instead.

There was a need for a decent guest house in Inishowen, especially with the increased business in the area amidst all the military activity. They spent some money on expanding and upgrading the premises. Catherine would take over the management of the business, and James would help out in the bar when he wasn't on the boat. As an added bonus, Catherine was able to build a studio at the rear of the premises where she could teach Irish music and dance, a thing she loved to do.

In an effort to suppress the Celtic Irish culture, the authorities outlawed the Irish language, including Irish song and dance. Catherine set up her studio under the guise of 'Scottish dancing' as nobody really knew the difference. The native Irish language was a real headache for the authorities, who spoke nothing but English. They couldn't speak it, nor could they understand it, while the Irish always denied any understanding of the English language, but most Irish knew enough to get by. This made it very difficult for the authorities to question or interrogate the native Irish.

James and Tony made a trip back to the Island together and collected Seamus's distilling equipment and his earthenware jars, which seemed to number in hundreds, and packed them all into a boat. Before they left, they took one last walk around the island just for old times' sake, and of course, they took one last swim in the sea. They loaded the equipment onto the 'Mary Rose,' secure in the chestnut tree below the captain's cabin and ready for the next trip to Scotland.

It was shortly after that the first shipment of beer and whisky and, of course, poteen arrived in Inishowen. The 'Thatch' finally opened under new management with a night of music, dance, and Seamus Mac Callan's homemade brew.

Malcom passed away later that year, and having no surviving children of his own, he left the shipping business to James on condition he would take care of his ailing wife, Evelyn. James looked after Evelyn like a son; this was his family away from home. The 'Mary Rose' continued to sail between Ireland and Scotland and was a frequent sight in the Inishowen headland. It wasn't long before the 'Thatch' became one of the busiest and most frequented Inns in the district. It catered to all the needs of the community.

It had separate meeting rooms for special occasions, whether it be a wedding or, a funeral wake, or just for privacy. The 'Thatch' became the hub for communication and news for the whole area. A place where rumors started and secrets were revealed, where messages were relayed, and where it was dangerous to get drunk and speak your mind. There was always someone listening, and there was always someone watching.

Whenever James could, he helped out at the 'Thatch' and spent a lot of his time attending the bar, especially during the winter months when he wasn't too busy on the boat. He sometimes felt like a priest hearing confession, with his customers sharing their problems and asking for his advice. He could never understand why people felt obliged to reveal their most intimate thoughts and secrets as well as their life stories when they were under the influence of Seamus Mac Callan's booze.

In time, he came to realize that the same information could get people arrested and, in some cases, even hung. These were dangerous times they were living in, and Seamus Mac Callan's booze was the one thing that helped his customers to relax and forget their troubles, but it also seemed to loosen people's tongues. James himself, being wholly aware of the consequences of loose talk, would always pass it off as drunken gibberish and not worth paying attention to, but others did.

They remembered every word, every plan, every betrayal, everything. Everyone had their ears cocked. Johnny Mac could hear a pin drop from across the room. The 'Thatch' became the intelligence center for the rebels and the militia alike, and James found himself in the middle of it all. People spoke in riddles and code. Sometimes in the Irish Gaelic and sometimes in the Queen's English. Signs and signals were commonplace, with the wink of an eye or the raising of an eyebrow. James felt it was his job to look after his customers and keep them out of trouble. He knew when to shut them up, when to interrupt, change the subject, and ensure everyone got home safe.

The militia were always carrying out house searches for rebels on the run or for arms and ammunition. They knew that the rebels had large amounts of stolen weapons but could never figure out where they were hidden. It was not safe to hide or store arms in a private house, so an alternative location was found.

Arms and ammunition were packed into coffins and buried in shallow graves in the graveyard where they could easily be retrieved when needed and easy to store and often done unknowingly with the church's blessing.

Besides, nobody was likely to go digging up bodies in a graveyard. The grave diggers were two brothers, Tom and Mick O'Brien. They were both rebels and staunch supporters of the cause. They saw to it that the rebels killed in action were secretly given a proper Christian burial in consecrated ground. You might say they knew where all the bodies were buried. 'Johnny Mac' would organize safe houses for rebels on the run, and when it was warranted, a trip to Scotland was arranged.

The nine years war between the Irish confederation of Irish chieftains and the Crown forces intensified when Red Hugh O'Donnell, the 1st Earl of Tir-Connell, who was the elected chieftain of his clan, escaped captivity from Dublin castle and made it home to his castle in Donegal. He was joined by the O'Dohertys, the O'Neill's, the Maguires, the O'Rourke's, the MacSweeneys, and many others. They won many battles and skirmishes against the forces of the Crown and drove them out of Donegal.

The Irish Confederation, under the leadership of O'Neill and O'Donnell, won a decisive victory, crushing the Crown's forces at the battle of 'Yellow Ford'. The Spanish monarch Philip was very supportive of the

Irish cause and sent an army of 3,500 soldiers with arms and ammunition, landing on the southern coast of Ireland in the small town of Kinsale.

The armies of O'Neill and O'Donnell marched south to meet them. The forces of the Crown, with an army of 7,000 strong, under the command of Lord Mountjoy, besieged the Spanish army at Kinsale and definitively routed the combined Irish rebel forces of O'Neill and O'Donnell.

The defeat of the Irish, who up to now owed their success to guerrilla warfare and ambush, was due to their lack of discipline in the ranks, and with very little if any battle experience, they were unable to form a proper squadron formation on the battlefield and when attacked, they panicked and fled for their lives. They were pursued and cut down by the cavalry, who followed them for miles. There was also a lack of trust between O'Neill and O'Donnell that resulted in a rivalry and a lack of discipline in the rank and file of the Irish forces. As a result of Hugh O'Neill's Protestant upbringing and his previous loyalty to the Crown, as witnessed by the Elagh Castle massacre of the Spanish shipwreck, he was not trusted by the other Irish Chieftains who regarded him as a leader to be devious, unreliable and egocentric.

After their defeat in the battle of Kinsale, the two earls, Hugh O'Donnell and Hugh O'Neill, returned to Ulster to protect their homelands. Red Hugh O'Donnell died shortly afterwards and was succeeded by his younger brother, Rory O'Donnell. The nine-year war ended with the signing of the

Peace Treaty of Mellifont by Hugh O'Neill on behalf of the two leaders. They were given a pardon and allowed to keep their titles and most of their lands, and in return, they pledged their loyalty to the crown.

However, when the two earls, Hugh O'Neill, and Rory O'Donnell, travelled to Europe to seek Spanish aid for a new rebellion to restore their power in Ulster, their action was declared treasonous, allowing the British Lord Deputy in Ireland, Arthur Chichester, to expropriate their lands and their titles and implement the Plantation of Ulster with tenants who were loyal to the King. When the Earls sailed from Rathmullen, on the shore of Lough Swilly and the Inishowen Peninsula, on an unnamed French warship for mainland Europe, a large number of boats, including the 'Mary Rose', lined the route to wish them a safe journey but also to lament their parting.

Unfortunately, Philip of Spain had already made his peace with King James, who succeeded Queen Elizabeth. Back in Ireland, the unsuccessful rebellion of Cahir O'Doherty in Derry left the way open for the Crown to implement a more radical plantation of north Donegal.

The city of Derry was given to twelve London companies and thus the name 'Londonderry.' The adjacent Barony of Inishowen was granted to Arthur Chichester, the Lord Lieutenant, for his part in suppressing the O'Doherty rebellion. He was not bound by the same regulations as the other Ulster Plantation undertakers, so he settled the peninsula with friends and family. The Inishowen peninsula, which was included in the parish of Derry by Bishop Gemanus, continued to coexist with the Protestant Church.

The plantation of Ulster was designed to create a community of English-speaking, non-Catholic, loyal British subjects to replace the barbarous and rebellious Gaelic-speaking Irish. The new landowners, most of whom came from Scotland and Northern England, were granted the best arable land while the native Irish were forced to farm the poorer marshy and rocky land.

The Protestant Church of Ireland received all the churches and lands previously owned by the Catholic Church. However, the majority of the Gaelic Irish remained in their native areas and worked hard to survive on the rocky land that nobody else wanted. Some of the new landlords could not import enough non-Catholic tenants and, in many cases, had to fall back on the Irish to work the land. Groups of Irish dispossessed of their land by the British rebelled and were known as wood-kern who constantly attacked and raided the new land settlements. The British set up fortifications to protect the new settlements in Derry and throughout the Inishowen peninsula. Life in Donegal and around the country in general became very difficult for the Native Irish Catholics.

Francesco had seen it all before in Switzerland and knew it was only a matter of time before the Protestant-controlled parliament would use its political power to extend its influence in Inishowen and the rest of Ulster.

The Catholic Church had been keeping a very close eye on the politics in Ireland and knew that sooner rather than later, the Catholic religion would be outlawed both in Ireland and England, church property would be confiscated, and catholic clergy outlawed and forced into hiding and prevented from administering the sacraments to the faithful.

They would discourage the use of the Celtic Irish language and customs. They would use whatever means possible to force Catholics to convert to the new religion of King Henry VIII.

Francesco knew that Anthony would not shirk or run from his duty to his Irish catholic community, no matter what. Francesco was proud of his sons and was not going to desert them when they needed him most. They may have to go undercover until things improved with time, as they always do.

Now was the time to prepare the groundwork if they were going to be ready to meet the challenges of the future head-on. The bishop arranged for Francesco to stay with an order of Franciscan monks. They established an affiliation between the order in Ireland and his own monastery back in Italy.

Anthony studied medicine so he could use this cover as a medic to get access to the sick and dying and allow him to administer the last rights. Catherine managed the 'Thatch' and organized classes for the local children, promoting the Irish culture where possible. James was always at hand to help in case a speedy exit was required; he was able to organize a trip to any part of Europe.

He would never forget the help he and his brother Tony got from Fr Pius on those treacherous days when they themselves were on the run. Catherine's family took over and worked the farm. James and Catherine kept a vegetable garden that supplied everyone with an abundant supply of produce when food was scarce. Gardening was the one thing they both really enjoyed.

The years passed without too much hardship. James and Catherine had their little nest egg to help them through the rough years that lay ahead. They had two more children before Catherine was told she could not have any more of her own. A girl they called Fiona and a boy named James after his father. Both grew up in the native Irish traditions and were fluent Gaelic Irish speakers with a love for the Irish culture.

Fiona took after her mother and loved to sing and dance. The boys liked to help out on the boat and someday hoped to become sailors like their father and uncle. Francesco was very friendly with the bishop and even accompanied him to Rome and met with the Holy Father. Francesco fell ill one summer and did not make it through to the fall.

He died with his two sons and family by his bedside. With James's help, some of Francesco's friends made the journey from Venice. He was buried under the willow tree next to Fr. Pius and Eileen, overlooking the Ocean. A stone was erected to mark the spot with an inscription.

"How you live your life, you'll find

Is greater than all else, left behind."

James and Anthony visit the grave site regularly, the resting place of Eileen, Pius, and Francesco, their three dear friends. Anthony still carries the gold cross with the relic of 'St Francis of Assisi' around his neck for protection but also to remind him of the journey that brought two young boys from the Alps in Switzerland to the sands of Inishowen in Donegal, Ireland. They had finally found their way back home—the home where they were always meant to be.